I0601312

Dark Secret

Michelle Escamilla

Dark Secret

Copyright © 2015 by Michelle Escamilla.
All rights reserved.
First Print Edition: November 2015

Limitless Publishing, LLC
Kailua, HI 96734
www.limitlesspublishing.com

Formatting: Limitless Publishing

ISBN-13: 978-1-68058-371-7
ISBN-10: 1-68058-371-9

No part of this book may be reproduced, scanned, or distributed in any printed or electronic form without permission. Please do not participate in or encourage piracy of copyrighted materials in violation of the author's rights. Thank you for respecting the hard work of this author.

This is a work of fiction. Names, characters, places, and incidents either are the product of the author's imagination or are used fictitiously, and any resemblance to locales, events, business establishments, or actual persons—living or dead—is entirely coincidental.

Dedication

To my wonderful friends and family.

Chapter One

Life had always been rather ordinary for Emma Blackwood. She did well in school, played lacrosse, and was even part of the debate team. She wasn't exactly popular, but she did have a few friends and still tried to have fun through high school. Her dad left when she was young, so Emma spent most of her free time at her mom's bookstore. She was raised by her mom and really enjoyed the relationship they had developed over the years. Since her dad wasn't in the picture, Emma never wanted to open up old wounds and bring up the subject of 'why' to her mom. She had assumed, that like most of her friends' parents, they had 'fallen out of love' and moved on.

Growing up in a small town, Emma had dreamed of living the 'big city' life. It wasn't small enough that everyone knew each other's names, but it sure felt close enough. Before Emma was born, her mom had lived in the city. She would try to convince Emma that the city wasn't as luxurious as it seemed. But this didn't stop her from grabbing the first college scholarship halfway across the country and heading out. Although leaving her mom was the hardest thing, Emma needed to escape.

Her freshman year of college, Emma felt like a social outcast. She had grown up with the same friends her whole life, so making new friends felt so foreign. During her freshman composition class, she had almost fallen down the stairs, but thankfully was rescued by one of the hottest men in her class, Kyle Anderson. Throughout the semester, they got to know each other a lot better. She was struggling through English, while he was having a hard time in his finance class—one that Emma seemed to master. After spending countless hours of time together, they tried to take their relationship to a whole new level. Awkwardly, they found themselves feeling more like siblings rather than boyfriend and girlfriend.

They made the best of their relationship and enjoyed just a friendship. Their college years were the best, even if it was just the two of them. During their junior year, after spending their first two years in the dorms and driving their roommates crazy, Emma found a small apartment they could just barely afford. Most nights were spaghetti leftovers or Cup of Noodles, but their fridge was always stocked with beer.

After graduation, Emma found a job at a local coffee shop while trying to find a 'grown up' job. Kyle began working at a small newspaper. It was shit money for the two of them, but they knew it was just a start. Emma's mom would constantly call to make sure they had enough money for the month and dropped several hints for her to move back home. After a week straight of SpaghettiOs, Emma had considered the offer, but couldn't imagine moving back to a small town. One day, Kyle finally got a promotion and things began to look up. Life wasn't going to be ordinary for Emma anymore.

***

"Emma! Pizza guy is here!" Kyle hollered from the kitchen.

"Oh, is it the hot one?" Emma shouted from her room while drying her hair with her towel. After spending the day on the couch, she finally decided that it was time to take a shower.

"I don't know!" Kyle scoffed.

"It's okay to think that guys are hot, Kyle." Emma giggled, tossing her hair into a messy bun on top of her head as she walked down the hallway toward the front door.

"And it's okay to have some hot girl-on-girl action." He chuckled.

"Touché, but unfortunately for you, it's not gonna happen. Can you hand me my wallet?" she asked, pointing to it on the counter. Kyle tossed it to her before grabbing a couple of beers out of the fridge. Emma opened the door, anticipating the blond hair, blue eyed, too hot to be delivering pizzas dream man, but instead found an older woman with stringy salt and pepper curls who looked like she hated life itself. Emma quickly handed her the money and grabbed the pizza before she made Emma hate life as well. While Kyle

3

grabbed plates out of the cupboard, Emma carried the pizza to the living room. For the last few years, since they had moved in together, this was their Friday night routine. Pizza, beer, and movies. Kyle had become rather popular with the ladies during senior year, but he made most of his 'dates' on Saturday nights.

"You know, we should be going out," Kyle said, stuffing a large bite into his mouth.

"I know, but...it's pizza night," Emma grumbled.

"Finish your pizza and then get dressed. I haven't been laid in four days!" Kyle stated before he took one last swig of his beer.

"Oh, you poor thing. Whatever will happen to you?" Emma joked, pulling a piece of pepperoni from her pizza and playfully taking a bite.

"Hey, I went thirteen years once." He smirked.

"Is that when you lost your virginity?" she asked, giving him a look of disgust.

"Yep."

"Whore. It's been months for me!" Emma sulked.

"Yep, again."

"And how would you know?" Emma scoffed, smacking Kyle's arm.

"'Cause I live with you, and you've bought more batteries in the last couple months than I have in my entire life." Kyle tried to hold back from laughing, but couldn't resist.

"You're an ass. Well, I'm sorry, but after the last guy..." Emma paused. Talking about Tyler would have only made her night shitty. She playfully

4

smacked Kyle once more before taking another drink of her beer. Tyler seemed like a great guy in the beginning, Emma and he had really hit it off. Except for the day when he told her he was sick and she went to take him some soup and Kleenex and found him with another girl in his bed.

"Let's not talk about that shithead. Either way, we're going out. So get your lazy ass up off the couch and go get ready." Kyle patted her leg, standing up from the couch.

Stuffing a rather large bite of pizza into her mouth, Emma growled at Kyle and sunk into the couch. Kyle had a determined look about him, so she knew this argument wasn't going to end in her favor. She mumbled to herself as she watched Kyle make his way toward his room.

Kyle was definitely a good-looking guy—tall, blond hair, and brown eyes. He had muscles, but they weren't overdone, and he sort of reminded her of Justin Timberlake. Whenever any of her friends would ask her why she wasn't with him, Emma would start to give them the whole song and dance about how great of a friend he was and how he was more of a brother to her. Emma's friends would zone out on her speech and quickly move in on him. Emma was almost one hundred percent sure that he had slept with all of her friends at least once. Unfortunately, as soon as he slept with them, he'd never call them again, so they rarely hung out with Emma for fear of having to run into him. Emma was destined to have Kyle as her only friend. She was okay with this, but really did miss girls' night out. Making her way to her room, she shut her door and began to plot her outfit for the evening.

"Emma, you have thirty more minutes," Kyle informed her, knocking on her bedroom door.

"Until what, you turn into a civilized guy?" Emma chuckled at her joke. She paused to listen for a laugh from Kyle. She didn't get one.

"No, smart-ass. We leave whether you're ready or not. Hurry up!"

Since being introduced to makeup her sophomore year of college, the thought of going anywhere without it wasn't an option. She quickly applied her eyeshadow and added a bit of lipstick. Looking over her outfit, black sequined top, skinny jeans, and her killer red heels, she felt pretty impressed with herself. "Damn, I'm hot," she whispered to herself.

"Wow. You look...human!" Kyle joked as she walked into the living room.

"Oh, shut up! Just because I've had time off from work, haven't put on makeup in a few days, and find the luxury of sweatpants appealing, doesn't make me non-human! So, do you like my haircut?" Emma had kept her hair long since she was little. Her mom rarely let her cut it and it just seemed so easy to throw it into a ponytail rather than try to style it. After a long funk, Emma decided it was time for a change. Her hair that once ran down her back was now up to her shoulders. It wasn't much of a change, but to her it was a lot of hair. She had even added a few highlights to try to vamp up her style.

"I kinda like it," he said skeptically.

"Only kinda?" Emma asked, batting her

eyelashes.

"Em, you're like my sister. I can't exactly say you look hot!"

"Umm...yes, you can!" she scoffed.

"Fine, you look hot. You ready?"

"Yep." Emma smiled. "Let's go."

Emma grabbed her handbag off the table and followed Kyle out of their apartment. Denver's nightlife was always a lot of fun. There was never really a dull moment downtown. Emma realized she was grinning from ear to ear as she saw her reflection in the window of the taxi. Even though she didn't have any expectations of meeting anyone, she was excited for the copious amounts of alcohol and dancing.

***

The bar was packed tonight. It had been months since the last time Emma had gone out, let alone consumed hard alcohol. When she started dating Tyler, he had told her that the club scene was not for couples and he didn't want to ruin their new relationship. He thought bars were only for people to go find someone to pick up for the night. It turned out that's exactly what he wanted, along with one of Emma's 'friends.' Emma wanted to drink away any memory of him tonight.

After several hours of dancing and allowing Kyle to choose her shots, Emma was practically lying on the table. "Do you know what I love?" Emma slurred to Kyle.

"No, what do you love?" he asked, running his

hand through his hair.

"I love…this drink." She beamed, taking the last drop onto her tongue. Emma was a lightweight when it came to drinking and tonight was no exception. When last call was announced, doubles of rum were ordered. Emma had lost count of how many drinks she had consumed. At some point during the evening, Kyle had found some busty blonde to chat up and brought her back to their table. She must've felt like she won the lottery since she had been trying to make her way over to him all night, but she didn't like the fact that Emma was with him. Kyle was not one to ditch Emma for any girl. Especially for a booty call.

"What I don't love…" Emma continued.

"Yep…" Kyle waited for her response, taking a drink of his beer. The blonde's hands were all over Kyle. He looked rather unimpressed with her.

"Fake boobs!" Emma blurted out, laughing. Kyle choked on his beer before both he and the busty blonde glared over at her. She grabbed her drink and huffed off when Kyle didn't defend her.

"Jesus, Emma, could you…I don't know, filter some of the shit that comes out of your mouth?"

"Sorry, I'm really drunk. I need to go home, please," Emma groaned, resting her head on her arms.

"Yeah, let's get you home," he agreed, taking the drink away from her. "Hang on. Can you manage to stay here for a minute? I gotta take a leak."

"Yeah, I'll wait. Right. Here," she groaned, standing up from the chair. Kyle sat her back down on the chair, making sure she didn't fall over.

Kyle made his way through the crowd toward the restrooms. Emma rested her head on her hand, watching the crowd make their way out of the bar. "All I wanna do is crawl into my bed and sleep for the next three days," she grumbled to herself. The room began to feel like it was spinning.

"Are you okay?" a deep voice asked, touching her back.

"Huh?" Emma asked, confused, looking for the owner of the deep voice. It didn't sound like Kyle.

"Do you need me to call a cab?" he asked, stepping to her side. She looked up to find a tall guy with jet-black hair studying her.

"Uh, no. M-my roommate just ran t-to the bathroom," she stuttered. This guy was amazingly hot. His gray eyes were so captivating, and all Emma wanted to do was stare at him for the rest of the night.

"Okay, I just wanted to make sure you were safe getting home," he insisted, touching her arm again before walking away. The hair on her arms stood straight, like an electric surge had coursed through her body.

"All right, Em, let's head out," Kyle said, helping her off the chair.

"Holy shit, did you see that guy?" Emma asked, looking around the bar for the mysterious man.

"No. Do you know him?" Kyle didn't bother to look around. His concern was getting Emma out of the bar without her puking on him.

"No, but I want to." She giggled, grabbing her purse off the table.

Kyle picked Emma up off the chair and carried

her toward the entrance. Their apartment wasn't far from the bar and they could've actually walked, but Kyle flagged down a taxi. "Em, I'm sorry, but at twenty-three, you should be able to handle your liquor a little bit better."

"I'm sorry," she murmured, followed by a hiccup. "Did Boobs McGee wanna come over?" She giggled.

Kyle laughed. "No, I think she'll be skipping our place tonight."

As they slid into the taxi, Kyle gave the address to the driver and Emma rested her head on his shoulder. She felt nauseous the entire ride home, so she closed her eyes to try to take her mind off of it. Visions of Mr. Tall, Dark, and Handsome flashed through her thoughts.

"Em, we're home," Kyle whispered, lightly shaking Emma awake.

"Ugh, okay," she groaned. Kyle once again picked her up and carried her up to their apartment. She could tell she was going to have sweet dreams about the mystery man, but the hangover in the morning was going to suck.

***

"Dear God, please make the beeping stop," Emma grumbled before the beeping of her alarm came to a stop. She raised her head to offer thanks to Kyle, but found an empty room. Her only assumption was that her alarm finally needed to be replaced. Nine in the morning was a brutal hour to wake up after a night out. Emma always considered herself a night owl, so anything before noon was brutal even if she had stayed in. Today, Emma didn't have to go into work until two in the afternoon, but she didn't want to spend the day in bed. The new plan for the day was to get a functional alarm clock.

She sluggishly pushed herself out bed. She could only think of two things: water and Advil. Padding her way to the kitchen, she found Kyle sitting at the table, sipping on his coffee as he looked through a magazine. "Good morning, Sleeping Beauty," he greeted her, looking up from the article.

"Ugh. Coffee," she responded in what sounded like English.

"There's Advil and some water waiting by the coffee pot for you," he offered.

"Thanks. Did I make a total ass out of myself?" she asked, pouring coffee into her mug.

"Nah, you didn't. However, you pointed out that you like the natural look more." Kyle tried to hide his smile.

"What?" Emma asked, confused, before popping the pills into her mouth and chugging the water.

"You made it well known that you don't like fake tits."

"Oh, shit. I'm sorry," Emma gasped, blushing. She took a seat in the chair next to Kyle at the table, taking a sip of her coffee.

"It's okay. I think I slept with her friend a week ago anyway. I don't need to get mixed up in that drama." Kyle tossed the magazine to the other side of the table.

"Wait. You think?" Emma looked at him

strangely.

"It was dark in the club and she wouldn't talk to me, so I'm only assuming." He took a sip of his coffee and looked at his watch. "Hey, you got work today?"

"Yeah, at two. Why? And why are you up so early?"

"Christmas is only a few weeks away, so I should probably go get some shopping done," he sighed.

"Shit, it's that soon? I probably should get some done too." Emma and her mom never really made a big deal of Christmas. Since it was only Kyle and her mom in her life, she never really had to do a whole lot of shopping.

"Are you going back home?"

"Yeah, wanna come with me?" Emma linked her hands together to beg him. Kyle was always a good distraction from her mom constantly asking Emma to come back home to live with her.

"I'd love to, but I'm actually heading home to see my mom," Kyle said, taking a swig of his coffee. He and his mom had a falling out a while ago, and then his dad passed away last year. Since then, she'd been trying to rekindle things.

"That's great. Well, I need to run to the store and buy a new alarm clock. Wanna go do some shopping together?"

"Yeah, I'll meet you in the living room in an hour?" he asked as he stood up and walked over to the sink to rinse his cup.

"Perfect. Lemme get a little bit of coffee flowing through my veins and then I'll grab a quick shower." Emma took another sip of her coffee as Kyle headed into his bedroom and closed the door behind him.

As Emma sipped on her coffee, wishing for her head to stop pounding, she tried to remember what other stupid shit she had said last night. "Fake boobs?" she asked herself, smacking her forehead. Nothing more had come to her mind except her mystery guy and the fact that he was so mesmerizing. Seeing how that was the only thing she could really remember from last night made her want to find out who he was even more.

Trudging her way back to her room, she began to get ready. She felt rather lucky as she looked around her room. When they were looking for places, they were supposed to have the unit one floor below them that was a two bedroom, but only one bathroom. Emma wasn't exactly keen on the idea of sharing a bathroom with Kyle and the harem he had, but it was something they could comfortably afford. On the day they were supposed to move in, the management office called them and asked if they would be interested in moving up one floor to a double master for only a hundred extra bucks a month. Kyle jumped on it and told Emma he would cover the extra cost. She couldn't say no.

As she stood in front of her bathroom mirror, Emma examined her hair. She was still in disbelief that she allowed herself to cut it. She asked Kyle what kind of style she should go for. He suggested she go Goth. He got punched.

As Emma stepped into the shower, the water pounding on her back actually felt soothing. She prayed the Advil would kick in while she stood under the water. She hated having a hangover.

Chapter Two

"All right, so I have just about everything I need. Did you find an alarm clock?" Kyle asked Emma as she browsed the through the nail polishes.

"Oh yeah, that's why I'm here. Oops. I need to go grab one. The lines are crazy long, do you wanna go grab us a spot?" she suggested, walking away toward the alarm clocks.

"Yeah, but hurry your ass up," Kyle said, walking toward the checkout lanes.

"Okay, Dad…" Emma sighed, rolling her eyes as she turned into the aisle. Browsing through the several different styles of alarm clocks, she grabbed the most generic model. As long as it got her ass out of bed and to work on time, she really didn't care if it could connect to her phone. She began to make her way toward the checkout when the alarm clock in her hand began to beep wildly and then die. Emma inspected the packaging, but nothing seemed out of the ordinary or faulty. She placed it back on the shelf and grabbed another clock, but suddenly all of the clocks began to beep. Emma looked around to see if she was on some sort of prank show. She quickly grabbed an alarm clock that wasn't going crazy and ran out of the aisle. Kyle waved to her from one of the long lines.

"Find one?" he asked as she approached him.

She showed him the package and placed it in the cart. "Can I just add this to your stuff? I'll just give you cash for it."

"Yeah, no prob. What happened? It took you forever." Kyle inched the cart closer to the counter and began to unload his few items of travel toiletries.

"The alarm clocks had all gone crazy!" She chuckled, grabbing cash out of her wallet and handing it to him.

"What do you mean?" He looked at her with a puzzled look.

"I don't even know how to describe it." Telling someone sounded crazier than the alarm clocks actually going crazy.

"Ummm…okay? Anyway, you wanna grab some lunch before work?"

"That'd be nice." Emma grabbed her phone out of her back pocket and checked the time. "Okay, I have plenty of time."

"What time do you have to go in?" he asked, handing the cashier his card.

"Two, but I need to still run home and grab my shirt. So, somewhere we can eat quickly."

"Subs?" he asked Emma, taking his card back with the receipt.

"Perfect." Emma grabbed their bags and headed out toward Kyle's SUV. The cold December air chilled Emma to the bone. She began to feel really thankful for heated, leather seats. Kyle's driving was that of a race car driver. They drove toward the sub shop, listening to the nineties station on his XM radio. Kyle's lead foot got them there pretty fast. Pulling up to the local sub shop, Emma didn't want to leave the warm seat, but her stomach had other plans.

To escape the cold, Emma ran toward the door. Kyle opened the door for her and followed her in. "Thank you, sir. What are you gonna get?" she asked, grabbing her stomach as it growled.

"Probably just the club sandwich." He paused, looking up at the menu. "What are you getting?"

"I like the roast beef," she said, taking a step forward to the ordering counter.

"Emma likes the beef," he chuckled.

"Umm…it isn't like I said sausage. Dumbass." Kyle rolled his eyes and placed their orders. "Are you buying?" she asked, reaching for her wallet.

"Yeah, I guess. I'm in the holiday spirit of giving," Kyle answered, pulling out his debit card.

"Aww, I love you." Emma gave him a small hug before grabbing their cups. As Kyle paid, she filled their drinks and found them a booth in the back. As she sat down, she began to daydream about Mr. Mysterious. After sitting in the booth for several minutes without a sign of Kyle, she made her way around the corner to find out what he was doing, especially with her food. Emma rounded the corner to find him chatting up some brunette.

She walked up behind him, tapping him on the shoulder, clearing her throat. "Can I get my food?"

"Huh?" Kyle quickly turned toward Emma.

"My food. If you're gonna be trying to get a booty call, I'd kinda like to eat." The brunette scoffed as Emma reached for the tray in Kyle's hands.

"Sorry, Em. Tiana, this is my roommate, Emma. Emma, this is Tiana, my, err…"

"His girlfriend," she interrupted, holding her hand out to shake Emma's.

Emma tried to hide the laugh that was building. She behaved herself and quietly shook her hand. Since when was Kyle even boyfriend material? Emma took the tray from him, smiled to them both, and made her way back to another booth. As she began to eat her sandwich, Kyle slowly took a seat across from her.

"So, when did you get a girlfriend?" Emma smirked, trying to mask the snicker by taking a bite of her sandwich.

"Shut up. Tiana is a DEFCON five clinger. I slept with her last week and now she's planning our apartment décor. We're definitely not together!" Kyle tossed a piece of lettuce in Emma's direction.

"Holy shit, that's really bad!" Emma gasped, tossing a piece of lettuce back at Kyle.

"Yeah, and she was asking what I was doing for Christmas. I had to inform her that I wouldn't be bringing her home to meet my mom." Kyle took a monstrous bite of his sandwich.

Emma began to choke on the bite of her sandwich as she laughed. "How'd she take it?"

"She left in a huff and told me not to call her again," he sighed, taking another bite of his

18

sandwich.

"Maybe you should do a background check on the chicks you sleep with," Emma joked.

"Smart-ass. Eat your sandwich."

Emma snickered as she continued eating. The thought of Kyle actually settling down with someone was something to laugh about for the rest of the day. After finishing the last of her delicious sub, she checked her phone for the time. She needed to head in to work. She'd recently taken a few days off, not for anything special, but just to be completely lazy. It really wasn't the best time to take off, especially since she would be spending seven days away with her mom for Christmas.

"Do you think you can give me a ride to work?" she asked, shoving her phone into her pocket and cleaning her crumbs from the table.

"No," Kyle deadpanned.

"You know, I'm glad we only remained friends."

"And why do you say that?" Kyle chuckled.

"'Cause you're an ass," she said, glaring at him.

"Em, you really are the greatest friend. You aren't afraid to tell me the shit that you're really thinking," he laughed.

Kicking each other underneath the table, they finished up and headed toward the entrance when Emma paused, rubbing her arms. She felt a sudden chill race down her spine. The hair on her arms stood up straight, just as it did when Mr. Dark and Handsome touched her arm.

"You all right?" Kyle asked, handing her coat to her.

"Yeah, just suddenly got cold," she answered,

slipping her coat on.

"You turned pale. You sure you're gonna be okay to go to work?"

"I gotta. I'm already on some people's shit list at work. I already took four days off, and then I'm taking more days off to go see my mom for Christmas. I just think I'm still feeling last night." Emma zipped up her jacket and walked outside.

Heading toward Kyle's SUV, the snow began to lightly fall. Emma tightened her scarf, trying to warm herself. This winter seemed to be colder than last. Kyle always managed to find the furthest parking space away from any of the places they were going to. Emma didn't mind it on the nicer days, but with the winter wind blowing in, she really hated his choice of spots.

"You were pretty wasted." Kyle laughed.

"Yes, I know. I don't think I'm gonna drink for a while." She sighed, leaning her head against the cold window.

"No, that's what got you like that. You don't drink for a while and you lose your edge, so *more* booze for you!" Kyle threw his arms in the air.

"Uh…no thanks," Emma groaned.

"Just trying to help," Kyle offered, unlocking the doors.

"How, exactly?" she asked, giving a puzzled look.

"Well…you don't want to end up like last night every time we go out. You keep drinking and you'll be able to walk out on your own."

"You care so much," she muttered, rolling her eyes.

"I know. Anyway, let's get you to work. Make people happy by serving them coffee," he said sarcastically.

"Hey, I like my job. Sometimes."

"Why don't you find a Monday to Friday job?" Kyle was always trying to get Emma out of the coffee shop. Emma was miserable working there, making shit money even after being there for a year.

"I'm looking. I just haven't been able to find anything." She lifted her head off the window, rubbing it to warm it up. She had hoped the cold would help subside the throbbing, but instead, it only made her forehead feel frozen.

Kyle opened the passenger side door for her, and then ran around to his side. It always seemed like he had everything figured out. She often wondered why her life couldn't be easier. Everything planned out. They began to drive toward the apartment, so she could grab her work shirt, and then they headed down the road to her job. She really hated being lectured on her place of employment, but he had a point.

***

During the holidays it seemed like everyone drank more coffee. Emma had never seen the shop so packed with customers. Casey, her co-worker, and she were switching back and forth between making drinks and working the register. Since it was a small shop, typically there only one of them working, but thankfully, for Emma's sanity, they both were scheduled for today.

"Emma, can I get an espresso?" Casey called out.

"Yep, just give me a second," she shouted as she started to brew some more home-roasted coffee. She quickly stopped when she thought that she heard the guy from last night at the counter. Turning to see if it was actually him at the register, acting a little too excited, she spilled half-and-half down the front of her apron. What made it worse, it wasn't him, and so she had just spilled cream down the front of her to only get a glimpse of a gray haired, middle-aged man.

"Em! I need an espresso!" Casey reminded her. Emma and Casey had never gotten along. They had one of those love-hate relationships, minus the love.

"Sorry, coming up," she apologized, grabbing a cup off the counter. Emma was never really good at making anything but a pot of coffee. Even working here for a little over a year, she was still horrible.

The rest of the day began to slow as the skies darkened. Emma swore she saw the mystery guy twice more during her shift. Her mind was really playing awful tricks today. During her break, she sent Kyle a text.

Emma: Hey, movies and beer tonight?

She needed something to take her mind off today, and getting lost in some mindless comedies, combined with good beer, was a perfect night. She chuckled at herself, swearing off beer earlier and then offering it a few hours later.

Kyle: Yeah. Zoe might be over later too.

Great. One of Kyle's many regulars. In Emma's opinion, Zoe wasn't the best girl for him. Emma wasn't even sure that Zoe had two brain cells.

Emma: Great, I'll pick up beer on my way home. Off at eight, see ya.

Shoving her phone into her bag, she relaxed in the back office and looked at the clock. Jesus, it was only four thirty. Why was it that the only thing she wanted to do was think about this mystery guy? It's not like he was a celebrity or anything special. Emma decided to close her eyes for a minute.

"Emma! Its five fifteen! What the hell are you doing?" Casey seethed, pounding on the door frame.

"What?" Her eyes darted toward Casey, who was standing in the doorway with his arms crossed.

"You've been back here for forty-five minutes! I could use my break and some help up here!" Casey yelled.

"Oh shit, Case, I'm so sorry! My head was throbbing and I closed my eyes for a minute to try to get rid of the headache, and I guess I...I'll be up in a second." Emma quickly stood up and rubbed her eyes.

He rolled his eyes, heading back to the front. Emma had never fallen asleep at work, especially when working with caffeine, and felt incredibly embarrassed. Making her way back up to the front, she took over for Casey as he grabbed a cup of coffee and went on his break.

While the customers started to slow, Emma began to clean up the counters. She went to reach for the bottle of cleaner that was clearly out of her reach, when it suddenly moved into her grip. Stopping everything she was doing, her eyes darted down to the cleaner in her hand. "Holy shit! What the hell was that?" she whispered to herself. She slid the cleaner back to where it had originally been and tried to do it again.

"Umm, excuse me. Can I get a medium coffee?" a dark, but familiar voice asked.

"Yeah, I'll…" She turned to find mystery guy standing at the counter. "Oh, it's you!" she exclaimed, almost spilling the damn cream.

"Girl from the bar, how are you feeling?" he asked.

"Better, thanks. Sorry, you wanted coffee." She fumbled with coffee cups, trying to hide her shaking hands. This man had some power over her—she felt extremely nervous around him.

"Yeah, thanks. Just a medium, or what do you call it? A *grande*?" he asked, smirking. Emma stood there staring at him with a huge grin. She was certain that she looked like a complete idiot, so she tried to clean up the counter. "So, do I just call you 'girl from the bar'?"

She giggled nervously. "No, I'm Emma."

"Way better than the first name." He smiled, placing his hands on the counter. He leaned in toward her and she could smell his cologne. God, he smelled good.

"And you are?" Emma asked, staring at his eyes.

24

"Micah." His gray eyes seemed to mesmerize her once again, and they seemed to stand out more than she had remembered. His black hair almost looked like it had been styled, but messily. She just wanted to run her fingers through it.

"Nice to meet you, Micah," she said nervously. "Here's your coffee." She couldn't stop staring at his mouth. His lips looked so soft. She began to picture his lips everywhere on her. As she held onto his cup, his fingers gently grazed hers. His hands were just as soft. Oh God, she was fantasizing about this man.

"How much?" he said, waving at her.

"On the house," Emma offered, blushing. She snapped out of her fantasy, completely embarrassed.

"Thank you. Well, have a good night." He smiled, heading for the door.

"Thanks, you too!" She waved, turning back to clean the counters. Well, at least now she had a name to put to the fantasy. What an awkward way to be remembered, though. She turned around, smacking her head for acting like an idiot.

"Emma?" She turned to see Micah standing at the counter again.

"Hi, did you forget something?" Emma asked quickly.

"I'd like to take you to dinner tomorrow night. Seven work for you?"

"Uhh…yeah, I think I can do that." Emma blushed again.

"Great. I'll meet you here. I'm looking forward to it." He smiled, revealing a dimple in his right cheek, before he turned and left again. Even though he had a leather jacket on, she could still picture the bulge of his muscles underneath. She couldn't stop thinking about the guy…naked.

Here she was, fantasizing about the guy all day, spilling shit on herself because she thought she heard his voice, and then there he was telling her that he was taking her to dinner. On top of that, she had inanimate objects sliding across the counter toward her. She really needed to stop going out with Kyle to nightclubs.

What a weird fucking day. Emma needed a beer.

***

After a long day at work, Emma stopped at the liquor store to grab the six-pack of beer she had promised. She was more than willing to pay the pay-per-view prices than stand in line trying to find something in the video shop. Besides, walking home in the snow was not ideal.

"Kyle, you owe me big time!" Emma shouted, walking through the door. She was so glad to finally escape the cold.

"Oh, yeah? Why's that?" Kyle asked, walking into the kitchen. He watched her dust the snow off of her jacket and kick off her snow-covered tennis shoes.

"'Cause it's snowing, and I had to walk home after the long shift I had, carrying beer. Yeah, it sucked horribly." She walked to him, holding her hands out to touch his face.

"It's snowing?" he asked sarcastically. "Sweet! I mean, I'm sorry." He smacked her hands away, dodging fingers that were bright red.

"So, I've decided that you're buying the movies." Emma cupped her hands and blew on them to try to regain normal body temperature to her poor fingers.

"Deal. Leftover pizza for dinner?" he asked, holding a plate of greasy pizza out for her.

"You're forgiven." She set the beer on the counter, grabbed two bottles, and handed one to Kyle. Taking her plate to the couch, she sat down, opened a beer, and took a quick swig. Nothing beat a slice of pizza with a cold beer. She propped her feet up on top of the coffee table. Kyle had the fire place on and she could feel the heat on the bottoms of her feet. She slowly began to regain feeling in her whole body.

"How was your day?" Kyle asked, sitting down next to her, pushing her feet off of the coffee table.

"Lonnnng, but guess what?" she said excitedly, tucking her feet under her.

"Casey finally came out?" Kyle joked, taking a sip of his beer.

"No! I have a date tomorrow night!" Emma clapped her hands.

"Wow, two points for Emma! Who's the guy?" Kyle gave Emma a high five.

Just as she was about to answer, there was a knock at the door. Kyle set down his plate and jogged to answer. In walked Zoe. Emma let out a loud sigh, shoving food into her mouth. She was wearing the lowest cut sweater, with a pair of hooker boots over her jeans. Her bleached blonde hair appeared to be meticulously curled at the ends.

Did she know that she was just coming over for movies?

"Hey, Emma. How are ya?" Zoe asked. She sounded so fake, as if she really cared. She was only here to see Kyle, and Emma was just in the way.

"Great. Thanks," she replied, continuing to stare at the TV. Maybe if she didn't look at her, she'd go away.

"Zoe, can I get you a beer or some pizza?" Kyle asked, heading into the kitchen.

"I'll take another beer!" Emma interrupted.

"Umm, I'll have a glass of water, please." She beamed at Kyle before she turned to face Emma. "So, Emma, how are things going?"

"Okay, I guess. Just working and getting ready to go back home for Christmas." Emma wasn't sure why she was having this conversation with Zoe. This was the most they had talked. Ever.

"That's great. Is, umm, Kyle…has he been doing any shopping?"

"Yeah, it's the holidays," Emma scoffed.

"I mean, do you know if he got me anything?" Her big brown eyes reminded Emma of Puss in Boots when he did his 'sad kitty' face. That cat was cute, but Zoe just looked slightly pathetic. She wasn't even with the guy and she was expecting a Christmas gift?

"Honestly, Zoe, I have no idea," Emma sighed before shoveling some more food into her mouth. A look of disgust crossed Zoe's face as she watched Emma. Kyle came back into the room with two beers and a glass of water. Emma grabbed one of the bottles from his hand and nodded.

28

"What movie are we going to watch?" Kyle asked, taking his seat.

"Something funny," Emma announced.

"Whatever you want," Zoe added, snuggling into Kyle. Emma swore if she saw them start making out, she'd probably lose her delicious pizza.

They ended up finding *Forgetting Sarah Marshall* on cable, so rather than paying for something on pay-per-view, Kyle left it on. Emma had seen the movie a million times, but still found it as funny now as she did the first time. Zoe looked unimpressed and Emma really wished she'd leave. Unfortunately, she must've read Emma's mind and wanted to defy her, so she began to lock lips with Kyle. Emma was the one who ended up leaving.

Shutting her bedroom door, she turned on her small TV and changed into her warm sweats and a flannel top. God, she hated winter. Snuggling into her bed, Emma changed the channel to find the rest of the movie. Just as she began to get comfortable, she had a minor panic attack. She had a date tomorrow night with an extremely hot man and she had no idea what she was going to wear. These were the times that she wished that Kyle hadn't slept with all of her friends. Emma needed some girly help to figure out what to wear on a date. She decided to go with the next best thing and picked up her phone.

"Hey, honey. Are you still coming home for Christmas?" her mom asked as soon as she answered the phone.

"Yeah, Mom. I'll be there on the twenty-second." Emma loved her mom, but she often thought she was a little too clingy. Granted, Emma was her only child and halfway across the country, so Emma cut her a little slack.

"I'm so excited to see you! How's work going?"

"It was really busy tonight, but that's what happens when the weather gets colder." Emma paused for a moment, she couldn't believe she had to ask her mom for some fashion advice. "Hey, can I ask you a question?"

"Of course, what's wrong? Do you need money?" her mom asked worriedly.

"No, I think I'm good for now. Actually, I have a date tomorrow night!" Emma said excitedly.

"Oh," she said. Her mom was often skeptical about dating, but that was only because Emma had one serious boyfriend in high school. One summer he had gone to Europe with his family, and Emma learned he wasn't as great as he claimed to be.

"It's okay, Mom, it's just dinner. Anyway, I was wondering what you'd suggest I should wear."

"Well, where are you going?" she asked. Emma didn't know at this point if her mom was just getting the details of the date or if she was asking to know what kind of restaurant it was.

Emma paused, trying to recall if Micah had mentioned where they'd be going. "I honestly don't know," she chuckled.

"Well, be safe and wear something nice. Maybe a dress with some nice tights and boots?" she suggested.

"Oh, I can do that! Thanks, Mom! How've you been?" Emma browsed through her closet, looking at her vast array of clothes packed into it. She decided it would be best to wait until she was off the phone. She wandered over to her bed and took a seat.

"I'm good. Bookstore has been a little busy, especially with the holidays coming up. Everyone buys books."

"That's good! Oh, Mom, it's late! I'm sorry, I didn't realize it's almost eleven there! I didn't wake you, did I?" Emma gasped as she set the time on her new alarm clock while checking the time on her watch.

"No, I'm just having a cup of tea and then I'm off to bed. So, we have ten more days until you come out. Do you need me to get you anything?" she asked Emma, yawning.

"Mom, I'm good. Thank you. I'm gonna turn in too. I have to be at work tomorrow at nine," Emma sulked.

"Okay. I love you, and have fun on your date. Be careful," she begged.

"I will, Mom. Love you too."

Emma hung up the phone and settled down under her massive comforter. Once again, her mind was on Micah, but this time it was full of dirty thoughts. His hands moving up her thighs, his lips covering every inch of her body. She wanted to taste him, feel him, and be wrapped around him.

Chapter Three

Emma was wakened from a delightful dream by the annoying sound of her alarm. How in the world was she ever supposed to function as an adult if she couldn't get her butt out of bed at a reasonable time? "Working on Sundays should be banned," she grumbled, pushing herself out of bed and sluggishly making her way to the bathroom.

As she turned on the shower and waited for the water to warm up, she quickly brushed her teeth. After the incident at work, it was killing her to know if it was just a coincidence or if she could really do magic. She set her glass across the counter and put her hand out, taking a deep breath. "Come here, glass," she summoned. Nothing happened. She felt like an idiot; maybe it was just a coincidence. She looked away and felt the glass suddenly touching her fingers. "Fuck! What am I doing? Kyle!" Emma screamed for Kyle from her bathroom entrance.

Kyle burst through the door, running into her bathroom. "What the hell, Em? Are you okay?" he panicked, rubbing the sleep from his eyes.

She giggled at the sight of him in his pink flamingo boxer shorts. Then remembered why she'd called him in here. "The glass…my hand…"

"What?" he asked, looking at her and then the glass. He tried to figure out what she was going on about.

"Just watch," she instructed, placing the cup on one end of the counter. She stuck her hand out and repeated, "Come here, glass."

"And what am I watching?" he asked impatiently, crossing his arms, leaning against the door frame.

"Hang on." They stood there for at least five minutes with nothing happening. Kyle sighed as he switched the leg he was leaning on. The glass began to dance on the counter and then rolled off onto the floor. "No, that's not what happened!" Emma exclaimed, picking the cup off the floor.

"Emma…this is stupid, you scared the shit outta me. I came running in here for nothing!" Kyle huffed.

"No, just…lemme try again!" she begged, placing the cup back on the counter and turned her head, closing her eyes. She could hear the glass on the counter shaking, and once again, the glass was in her hand. She opened her eyes, quickly looking at Kyle.

"What. The. Fuck." Kyle looked at her in awe.

"I don't know. I did it at work last night and I thought it was because I was hungover!" She placed the glass on the counter, turning back to Kyle.

"You've never been able to do this before?"

Kyle asked, and Emma gave him a look.

"Kyle, do you think if I could do this before that I would just be telling you this shit now?" She smacked his arm. "Yeah, I'm going to keep this a secret from you!"

"That's so fucking weird!" He walked over to the counter, picked up the glass, and inspected it.

"What are you doing?" she asked, watching him look at the glass.

"I dunno, looking for something on the glass to say that this was a horrible magic trick," he joked. Before Emma could say some witty comeback, both were startled by stomping coming toward them.

"Kyle?" Zoe, with her 'just been fucked hair,' came wandering into the room. "What are you guys shouting about?"

Kyle quickly turned around to face her. "Sorry, Zoe, go back to my room. I'll be there in a second," he insisted, pushing her out of the bathroom.

She rolled her eyes and stomped back to Kyle's room, slamming the door.

"She's definitely not a morning person," Emma joked, taking the glass from his hand and placing it back on the counter.

"No, she's not. I think you should wait before telling anyone else about this," he suggested as he walked out of the bathroom.

"You're not kidding! I don't want to be locked up in the crazy house! You're the only one." Emma quickly followed him out of the bathroom.

"Just until we, better yet, *you,* can find out, uhh…what to call it." He stopped at her bedroom door.

"Definitely," she agreed, watching Kyle start to walk down the hallway.

"You workin' today?" he asked, turning around before he opened his bedroom door.

"Yeah, I was about to get in the shower. I have a date tonight, so I'll be home briefly to change clothes." Emma did a dance and Kyle gave her a look, shaking his head.

"All right, I'll see ya later." Kyle saluted.

"Have fun getting back to Sleeping Beauty." Emma laughed. Kyle flipped her off before walking back into his bedroom.

After wasting what could possibly have been gallons of water, she began to quickly wash up and finally got out. Emma browsed through all of her dresses, pulling out her black, long-sleeved dress and black tights and laid them out on the bed. She stared at the shoes in her closet. Since Micah was around six feet, she decided wearing heels was going to be a must. Emma ended up going with her knee-high, black, heeled boots.

As for work, she slipped on a pair of jeans with the company shirt. This was the best part of the job—the effortless outfit. She dug for her pair of tennis shoes in her closet, remembering that she took them off at the doorway the previous night because of the snow. Tossing her hair into a low side bun, she grabbed her scarf off the back of the chair and dashed into the living room.

Eight forty-five. She was almost always right on time for work, but had a feeling she was going to be a little late today. Slipping on her tennis shoes, coat, and scarf, she bolted out the door. Thankfully, she had a set of stairs and a hallway before she had to brave the cold. Approaching the door, she paused, taking a deep breath. She wasn't ready to go outside. As she headed out the door, Emma cringed as the cold hit her face. "Shit!" Emma screamed, almost slipping on her ass. You had to love three inches of snow covering a sheet of ice. Thankfully, work was only a few blocks away.

The last block and a half, she felt like she was running. She needed to get inside where it was warm. Emma quickly pushed open the door and rushed inside. "Nine on the dot, nothing like cutting it close," Casey scoffed.

"Good morning to you too, Casey. I didn't think you were in early today," Emma huffed, walking toward the back office. Removing her scarf and coat, she stopped when she realized Casey was following her.

"Miranda called in sick, so I had to open. I'm leaving around noon," he declared.

"Wait, what? I'm supposed to leave at three," Emma whined. It never failed, she was always the one to get the short end of the stick here.

"Well, now you get to close." He smirked, walking away. Emma wandered to the back office. Wow, someone had their Cheerios pissed on this morning. So, she'd get more hours, no big deal. She placed her things in a little locker that was set up in the back. However, that meant she'd only have an hour to primp herself before meeting Micah. Fuck. Slipping on her apron, she walked back out to the front and started to brew a new pot of coffee. It was going to be a really long morning if Casey was going to be pissy. Emma decided it would be best to distance herself from him.

"Good morning, Emma," a deep, male voice purred.

She quickly turned to see Micah standing in front of the counter, again. "Hi. Good morning. How are ya?" She was excited to see him first thing in the morning.

"I'm good, thank you. We're still on for tonight?" He leaned in toward Emma.

"Yes!" she said a little too excitedly. She cleared her throat and tried again. "I mean, yes, if you are?" She needed to stop talking.

Micah chuckled. "Yes, we are." He stopped, pulling a ringing phone out of his pocket. "Excuse me, Emma, I need to take this. May I get a medium coffee, please?"

"Sure." She smiled, turning to pour a cup of coffee for him.

"Ma'am, can I get a cappuccino?" an older lady asked. Emma quickly snapped out of her mini trance and faced the lady.

"Yep, coming right up." Emma put the lid on Micah's coffee and set it on the counter, then made the cappuccino. "Two dollars and eighty-five cents, please." Taking the money from the lady, she watched Micah on his phone outside the café. He didn't look happy about the phone call. Once the call ended, he shoved the phone into his pocket and huffed back inside. "Bad news?"

"No, just…it's nothing," he sighed.

Holding out her hand, not even thinking about what she was doing, the coffee cup slid toward her.

She looked in horror at Micah, but it appeared he'd missed it. Emma sighed in relief. Though that would've made for some interesting first date conversation.

"Here ya go, one medium coffee." Emma held up the cup. His fingers lightly touched hers and her heart began to race. The hairs on her arm stood up.

"Thank you. So, I'll pick you up at your place tonight," he insisted before taking a sip of his coffee.

"Uh. Okay." She blushed, picking up a scrap piece of paper and writing down her address.

"What time are you off?" he asked, looking at the address before shoving the paper into his pocket.

"I have to stay a bit later than originally planned, but I'll still be ready by seven."

"Perfect. I'll see you then," he said, smiling.

Emma stood at the counter and watched him walk all the way out in total awe. The man was just oozing sex and *he* wanted to take *her* to dinner.

***

Six o'clock couldn't come fast enough. Emma wished they were as busy as yesterday because it would've made for a quick day, but she wasn't so lucky. Casey seemed to lighten up after his short break, which was a nice change from having to listen to his bitching.

People around the area were kind enough to lay salt on the sidewalk and the snow melted throughout the day. It did, unfortunately, get really cold once again. While walking home she was wide awake as the cold air nipped at her face. As the wind started to pick up, Emma was more than happy to see her apartment building up ahead.

"Hey, I thought you'd be home this afternoon," Kyle said, opening the door for her.

"Yeah, I thought so too, but a girl called in sick and then Casey had to cover, which left me to close. Oh my God, I'm so hungry!" Emma whined, slamming cabinet doors as she searched for something to eat.

"Didn't you eat?" he asked as he watched her grab a granola bar off the counter.

"I had snacks, but nothing official. I'm supposed to get ready for my date, like now, though. I'm going to look like a pig." She shoveled a large bite of granola bar into her mouth.

"So, you'll look like yourself?" Kyle said, cringing as he watched her devour the snack bar.

She shot him an evil glare as she walked down the hall, kicking off her shoes. "You're *hilarious*," she shouted sarcastically, trying to hold the food in her mouth.

"Is he coming to pick you up?" Kyle asked, following her down the hall.

"Yep, so that means you better be on your best behavior!" Emma scolded.

"I'm always on my best behavior. But let him know that if he hurts you, I'll break his face." Kyle started beating his fist into his other hand.

"Since when are you in the face breaking industry?" She chuckled, raising her eyebrow at him.

"Since Tyler," Kyle said seriously.

Of all the nights to be reminded of the asshole, he had to bring him up tonight? Emma plugged in her straightener and walked out of her room to find Kyle standing by her door. "You don't have to worry about me, I'm a big girl."

"I know you are, but you're my best friend and like a sister. Tyler really hurt you and I can't see you go through that again." No matter how much of an ass Kyle was, he was truly sincere with Emma.

She wrapped her arms around Kyle's neck and pulled him in close for a hug. Kyle had to be around the same height as Micah, so she pushed herself up onto her tiptoes.

"What are you doing?" he asked.

"Making sure my boots are going to be high enough." Emma snickered.

"You ruined a nice moment by figuring out shoes?" Kyle pushed her away.

"Sorry, I wanna look hot." Emma batted her eyelashes at him and gave him an innocent smile.

"Em, you're what, five-foot-nothing? You can wear ten-inch heels if you want."

"Shut up, I'm five-five. Look, all that aside, I appreciate you looking out for me." She glanced down at her watch. "Shit! I have fifteen minutes to get ready! When he comes, will you please, *please* be nice?"

"Yeah," Kyle answered dryly.

"Thank you." Emma beamed, smacking his face. Rushing back to her bathroom, she tried to straighten out her mess of a hairdo.

While she was applying one last coat of mascara,

Kyle knocked on her bathroom door. "Prince Charming is here."

"Were you nice to him?" she asked, tossing the mascara into her makeup bag.

"Yeah, I told him you were ill and couldn't go out," Kyle said seriously.

"What? Are you fucking with me?" Emma had a moment of panic.

"Yes," he chuckled. "I think that you need to get laid, er, I mean, go out."

"You're an ass. I'll be out in a minute. Offer him a beer," she instructed.

"Yes, Your Majesty." Kyle bowed to her as they flipped each other off. He turned and headed back to the kitchen.

Making sure everything was in place, Emma quickly tidied up her room and made her way toward the living room. Both the guys were laughing over some television program showing internet videos. Ah, male bonding. Good sign. She cleared her throat as she walked into the room.

"Wow. You look beautiful," Micah said, standing up from the couch.

"Thanks, you look…hot." She blushed at the words that just came out of her mouth.

"Thanks," he chuckled. "Let's go?"

"Yes." Emma turned back to Kyle and smiled. "Kyle, I'll see you later."

"You two behave. Em, I'll put some condoms in your nightstand," Kyle announced, smiling widely.

Micah smiled. "Thanks, Kyle. I think I've got that covered."

Emma blushed again, mouthing 'Fucker' to Kyle

41

before quickly turning back to Micah. Did he just assume she was going to give in to every single craving she had for him? Shit, he was kind of an ass. He held up her coat, allowing her to slip her arms into the sleeves, and then opened the door for her. They waved back to Kyle before making their way down the flight of stairs to his car.

A beautiful black Lexus RX waited right out front. He pressed his remote that started the car as they walked down the front stairs. She was glad that she chose the knee-high boots, as it was fucking cold out tonight. Micah opened the door for her, pressing a button on the side of the seat. Oh great, he had heated seats too! She was mentally noting if she were to break down and purchase a vehicle, it had to have these amazing heated seats.

"You ever been to Beatrice Woodsley?" he asked, settling into the SUV. He turned the heat to full blast.

"No, but I've only heard good things." On her salary she wasn't able to make it there. She still had to mooch money off her mom occasionally, so five-star dining was never going to happen.

"Good, that's where we're going." He placed the car into drive and sped off away from her building.

"Great!" she said excitedly.

As he drove to the restaurant, she couldn't help but sneak peeks at him. His gray eyes really stood out, even in the dark. He smelled amazing too. As she watched him drive, his hand slid onto hers. This was a great start to the night.

Chapter Four

The restaurant décor was something Emma had never seen before. Trees were actually in the dining room with bamboo covering the walls. It was beautiful. The food was equally impressive. She had been trying her hardest the entire meal to not stuff her face, but it was delicious and she was starving. Micah and she really didn't talk, which made this 'date' a little awkward.

"How was everything?" Micah asked, breaking the silence.

"Oh. My. God. I don't think I could eat anymore even if I tried," she said, grabbing her stomach.

"So...no dessert?" He smiled cheekily.

"Hmm...split?" Emma always had room for dessert. Kyle would joke with her, saying she was like a cow—not that she was fat, but that she had two stomachs.

"I think I could handle that." Micah waved the waiter over to their table as he looked over the dessert menu. After a meal like that, she didn't think she would ever be able to have frozen food ever again. Everything they ordered was paired with a different glass of wine, which brought out new flavors. It was incredible how each flavor was like a new food-gasm in her mouth. Everything seemed to melt on her tongue. Emma was in a semi-food coma as Micah ordered them dessert. As their waiter disappeared into the kitchen, Micah slid his chair over toward Emma.

"Hi, you okay?" he asked, smirking. His dimple flashed, making Emma's breath hitch.

She nodded, smiling widely at him. Her entire body tensed up and her heart began to race.

"I need to tell you something," he said, grabbing her hand.

"Oh shit, you have a girlfriend?" She pulled her hand away, but he quickly pulled it back.

"No," he said sternly.

"Oh...a boyfriend?"

"Did I give you a gay vibe?" he asked, surprised.

"No!" She felt embarrassed for even asking. "What would you like to tell me?" she asked.

"I can't stop thinking about you. Since I saw you at the club the other night, you've been stuck on my mind."

Her eyes widened as she couldn't believe what he was saying to her. The very guy she had fantasized about for the last couple of nights was now telling her he did the same thing. Emma wanted to say something, but all that came out was air. He leaned in, pulling her head close to him, and pressed his lips onto hers. Hard. He tasted of wine and some sort of spice, cinnamon, possibly. Either way, his lips were as soft as she had imagined.

44

Their waiter came back to the table, setting the dessert down as he cleared his throat. Micah's lips slowly pulled away from hers, but she kept her eyes closed in fear that she was actually dreaming. Her lips were met with the taste of chocolate and she slowly opened her mouth as Micah fed her a bite. She let out a soft moan.

"Good?" he whispered.

"Mmhmm." Before she could wipe any of the crumbs that didn't make it into her mouth, Micah leaned in and kissed them away. Emma swore she was on the brink of having an orgasm in the middle of a five-star restaurant.

"You're right, that is delicious," he breathed. She slowly opened her eyes, enough to just stare deeply into his hypnotizing eyes. "You about ready to head out?"

Once again, she only nodded her head as Micah signaled the water for their bill. Before the waiter could place the tab on the table, Micah handed his card to the waiter. He didn't even bother to look at the amount. Emma took the last sip of her wine before they headed out of the restaurant.

As they approached his car, he suddenly pushed her against the cold metal, kissing her intensely.

"You taste so good," he groaned.

Emma seriously melted right there in the middle of the parking lot. He started to kiss her again. As he gently parted her lips with his tongue, they heard a rumble of thunder across the skies. His kiss became fiercer, and another crash roared over them. His right hand scooted down her thigh before he reached around and squeezed her closer to him.

45

Emma's hands combed through his hair, and as she moaned into his mouth, a flash of lightning lit up the sky.

"Seriously, what month is this?" she asked, breaking away from his mouth. His lips traveled down her neck. The thunder and lightning suddenly disappeared and it began to snow.

"It's *you*," he whispered into her ear.

"Huh?" she asked. Did she hear him correctly, did he say it was her?

"Nothing. Let's get you home."

"Oh, okay." Emma was really confused, but didn't want to push the matter. Micah opened the door for her, pressing the heater button for her seat. She was no stranger to men, but this one did something to her that she'd never felt before. She didn't think she'd ever wanted someone so badly. Granted, she'd only slept with three guys, but she had never felt this sensation before.

The drive home was awkwardly silent. Did she have bad breath from dinner? She nonchalantly slipped a mint from the restaurant into her mouth, praying that this wasn't going to be the last she'd see of Micah. They pulled up to her building and sat outside, silently; still. Emma was getting impatient to taste his lips again, but she was slowly taking the hint. "Hey, Micah, this was fun. Thank you so much."

"Em, wait. I'm sorry," he spoke up.

"No, I understand. I'm not really your type after all. I do appreciate dinner, though." She reached for the door again.

"Wait, what? No, I'm totally into you! It's

just…I really wanna go up with you, and fuck you. Hard. But, I think that we should…wait," he said hesitantly.

Her mouth dropped open as he turned to face her. His eyes looked so dark. "Uh…I don't even know what to say to that."

"Say that you understand and we will definitely get together again. Real soon," he said as he smiled.

"I understand, and I'd love to see you again," she sighed. She was doing a happy dance in her head. This man wanted to see her again.

"Great. I'll call you," he stated.

"No, you probably won't," Emma teased.

"Why's that?" Micah looked at her with a puzzled look.

"'Cause you still have yet to ask for my number."

"Oh, yes. Sorry. Can I get your number?" he asked, looking surprised.

Emma pulled his cell phone from his jacket pocket and punched her number in. She leaned in and kissed his cheek, lingering a bit before she opened the door. He jumped out of the car and ran over to her. "What are you doing?" she asked, surprised.

"At least making sure you get upstairs okay." He pressed the lock button on his remote, then slipped the keys into his jacket.

"Okay." She smiled.

He helped her up the stairs, walking her to the door. She stood there for a moment before digging for her keys. As she was putting the key into the lock, Micah pulled her to the side. "I seriously think this could be a good thing, for you. For me."

"Please, come inside," she begged.

"I can't. Not tonight, but I just want to taste your lips. One. More. Time." His lips softly pressed against hers. They still had a hint of chocolate that made her want to cover him in that chocolate, and eat it all off his body. Her heart was beating uncontrollably, any faster and it was going to beat out of her chest. She swore she heard another rumble of thunder, but didn't want to ruin the moment again by mentioning it.

"Emma?" Kyle asked, opening the door.

Slowly pulling away from Micah, she looked over at Kyle, who was smiling like an idiot. "Yes?" She waited for him to respond. She really wanted to punch him for interrupting one of the greatest goodnight kisses.

"I heard someone at the door...are you okay? Your face is all flushed," he joked.

"Yep, I'm fine." She glared at him, hoping at that moment he could read her mind.

"Well, sorry to have interrupted," Kyle said, smirking. He stood there as if he were a big brother, waiting for her to come inside the house.

A moment of awkward silence passed over them. "All right, Kyle, I'll be just one more second." Emma shooed him back inside, closing the door behind him.

"Emma, I'm gonna go. I do want to see you again. Soon," Micah said, kissing her hand.

"Me too, Micah. Thank you again for tonight." She opened the door, waving to Micah as she watched him walk back down the hall.

"Wow, he's just gonna leave?" Kyle teased as Emma walked in through the door.

"Well, smart-ass, if you hadn't interrupted, I'm sure he would've come in!" she said, smacking Kyle on the arm. "Why are you still waiting by the door anyway?"

"Just making sure you made it in okay."

"Yep, believe it or not, I know how to open a door." She now understood the term 'blue balls,' and even though she didn't have the balls to turn blue, she was definitely feeling sexually frustrated.

"Hey, wanna watch a movie?" Kyle suggested as she took off her coat, setting it on the back of the kitchen chair.

"Not with another one of your skanks." Emma rolled her eyes, grabbing a glass from the cabinet for some water. He waited for her to fill up her cup and he walked into the living room.

"No, just you and me. I have to work in the morning and I don't want to have anyone over tonight," Kyle hollered as he sat down on the couch, grabbing the remote.

"Yeah," she sighed. "Lemme go change. What are you going to put on?" Emma took a big gulp of water and placed the glass in the sink before walking into the living room.

"I was thinking *A Tale of Two Titties*? Maybe some *Pulp Friction*?" Kyle laughed.

"Eww, you're such a dick! I don't wanna watch porn! It's only going to make things worse!" she sulked.

"All right, how about *Spaceballs*? You can't go wrong with Mel Brooks."

"Okay, I'll be out in a minute." Emma grabbed her coat off the back of the chair. Making her way into her bedroom, she threw herself onto the bed. What a fucking night! If she'd thought Micah was on her brain before, after those kisses it wasn't going to be easy to keep him off it now. She sighed as she undressed; she could still feel his hand along her side. Slipping on her sweats, she made her way back into the living room.

"Beer?" Kyle offered, grabbing a bottle off the coffee table.

"Please," Emma breathed.

"Hey, how's your new party trick?" he asked excitedly as he opened the bottle. "Did you figure out what it is?"

"Yes, it's a disease called 'I have no fucking clue.'" Emma laughed.

"Do you think penicillin could cure it? I know a buddy from college, he had to take that once and cleared him up real quick. Now he says his condoms are like his American Express."

"You boys are stupid. Seriously, though, I don't know what it is. Somehow I managed to get tomorrow off, so I'm gonna do some research. I mean, it's really weird that all of a sudden I can make objects come to me, right?" Emma and Kyle both took a swig of their beer and pondered on the whole situation.

"Hey, wanna go out to lunch tomorrow?" Kyle changed the subject.

"Really? Sure."

"My boss is taking a few of us and our 'others' out for lunch tomorrow and yeah, I don't have an 'other.' So, if you could be my date for lunch, I'd owe you big time."

"Why don't you take Zoe?" Emma joked.

"Seriously? You're passing up a free lunch?" Kyle looked at her, surprised.

"No! I was just wondering. You guys seemed kinda cuddly on the couch." The thought made Emma slightly sick to her stomach.

"Nah, she's amazing in bed..." Kyle began.

Emma held up her hands. "I really don't want to hear about how she is in bed, I might be sick," she warned.

"No, you should see what she can do! Either way, she's more bedroom material than boss luncheon material."

"Aww, Kyle Matthew Anderson! You think I'm boss luncheon material? I'm flattered! You know your bedroom girlfriend was trying to find out if you're getting her a Christmas present."

"Seriously? We've slept together *maybe* a total of...okay, I lost count, but have probably seen each other only a few times. I didn't know it justified a gift!"

"Are you getting *me* something?" Emma hinted.

"Maybe." Kyle smirked.

"Oh shit, I was just kidding!" Emma looked at him, surprised. They typically would take each other out for lunch or dinner for their gifts, so they never got each other something.

"No, you weren't. I got you something small, but I'm not giving it to you until I get back. When do you leave?" Kyle chugged the last bit of his beer.

"I leave the twenty-second and get back on the

twenty-eighth. Are you gonna be back for New Year's?"

"Sorry, I'll be gone from the twenty-third until the second. New York for New Year's!" Kyle put his hand up for a high five, but Emma shot him a look instead.

"Seriously? I'm so jealous! So, I guess I'll be all *alone* for New Year's Eve," she sulked.

"Maybe you can get...what's his name again?"

"Micah?"

"Yeah, him! Maybe you can get him to put out," Kyle laughed.

"God, you're a douche." Emma rolled her eyes, trying to hide her smile.

"I know, but you love me." Kyle hugged her tightly. She really did love him.

"Yeah, enough to tell you that I need you to drive me to the airport." She laughed as he pushed her away.

"I planned on it. All right, so lunch tomorrow, yeah?" Kyle started to push himself off the couch.

"Yes. Hey, where you going?" Emma asked, watching Kyle stand up. "I thought we were watching a movie."

"I'm exhausted. Wanna watch a movie in my room?"

"So you can fall asleep? Nah. I'm gonna head to bed too. If I'm going to be boss material, I need my rest and time to primp. Should I dress up?"

"As long as you don't wear your work jeans and tee, I think you can wear just about anything. I'll leave you some cab money, okay?"

"Aww you're so sweet."

"Night, Em." Kyle waved to her as he walked into his room.

"Night." Emma waved.

Although she really wanted to remove her ass from the couch, she couldn't stop flipping through channels as she tried to come up with a nice gift for Kyle. They'd never really exchanged nice gifts before, well except one year and he did buy her a new sheet set, but that was after his flavor of the week puked all over her bed. What do you get a guy's guy? One who actually gets everything and everyone he wants? She could order him a hooker, but that was way out of her price range and she didn't need any more skanks coming to their place. She had an idea, so she flipped off the television and ran to her room.

"Please say they're coming to town," she whispered to herself, booting up her laptop. Kyle had always been a big fan of Maroon 5, so finding tickets would be the perfect gift. "Yes!" she shouted, then covered her mouth. She pulled out her debit card from her purse and purchased two tickets to their next concert. She was stoked that she was able to find them. She did a little dance before throwing herself onto the bed and burrowing under the covers. She couldn't wait to dream about Micah.

Chapter Five

"Spread your legs a little further," he whispered into her ear. "Yes, like that." Micah's hand slowly moved up and down her thigh before tying her ankles down to the footboard, her wrists were already bound to the headboard.

"Please, I want this," she begged.

"I know you do. Once you tell me all of your secrets, we can have a lot of fun together." His voice sounded cold. So cold.

He began to kiss her calf, moving up her leg. Her back began to arch as he teased her clit with his tongue. She cried out, feeling so close to losing herself. "I don't know what secrets you want to know," she moaned.

"I saw what you did at the coffee shop, the thunder, it's not just a coincidence. I know your secrets, Emma. But you need to tell me what you know."

"I don't know!"

"Emma, I want to be with you. We can be amazing together, but you have to admit what you

are."

"What am I?" she moaned.
"A witch."

***

"Emma! Wake up!" Kyle shouted, shaking Emma awake.

"Huh? Kyle? What's going on?" She breathed heavily, quickly sitting up. She wiped the tiny beads of sweat from her forehead.

"I was just going to ask you the same thing. I heard you moaning from my room!"

She blushed, rubbing her eyes. "Oh shit, I'm sorry. I must've been having a nightmare."

"You think? But it did sound kinda hot...are you a screamer, Em?" he joked, nudging her with his elbow.

"Jesus, Kyle, it's the middle of the night and you're asking if I'm a screamer?" Emma asked, running her fingers through her hair.

"Middle of the night? It's seven fifteen," he said, showing her his watch.

"Wow...it feels like I just fell asleep. Even so, it's only seven in the morning and you're asking these questions? Go to work," she ordered, throwing herself back onto the pillow.

"I'm going. Cash is on the table and lunch is at one. Just come by the office, please don't be late," Kyle begged. He stood up from the bed and began to walk toward the door. Her heart was still racing from the dream.

"Yes, sir." She saluted.

"See ya." Kyle started down the hall, grabbing his bag off the floor.

"Bye." Emma waved before sitting back up. "Hey, Kyle?"

"Yes, coffee is made and still warm," he hollered as he made his way toward the front door.

"You really are the best!" Emma shouted, grabbing her robe. "What a fucking intense dream," she whispered to herself. Shaking her head, she chuckled at the thought of being a witch.

Pouring a cup of coffee, she tried to see what else she was able to do. Obviously she was capable of bringing things toward her. She began to 'reach' for the fridge from several feet away, and the door suddenly flew open. "Holy fucking shit!" she screamed, running toward the fridge. She grabbed the cream out of the door and slammed it shut.

Maybe her mom would know something about what was happening. She was a bookworm and had several books in her store that were a little off the wall. Emma didn't want to ask her about this shit over the phone, but could she wait a week and a half? Grabbing her cup of coffee, she walked back to her bedroom and grabbed her phone, dialing her mom's number.

"Hey, sweetie, how was your date?" she answered.

"It went really well…" Emma let out a quiet sigh, she couldn't tell her mom how hot and sexy Micah was. Let alone the fact that she had the most intense dream where he was tying her to his bed.

"That's great. So, I'm really excited to see you. It's been too long."

"I know, Mom." It really had been too long. Emma hadn't been home in almost a year now. It was really hard to leave her mom in the first place, but she'd had to escape.

"Any chance of you staying with me for good? You've been gone for too long," her mom begged.

"No, sorry. Maybe you can move out here! It's really nice and you'd love it," Emma hinted.

"Thanks, hon, but I love my home. Maybe I can bribe you to stay. I've got homemade cookies," she chuckled.

"Umm...as tempting as that is..." Emma started, but she knew that they were going nowhere with this conversation. Her poor mom. After that, she didn't even know how to approach the subject that she originally called her for, so she decided to leave it until she saw her.

"You okay, did you need to talk?" her mom asked her worriedly.

"No," Emma sighed.

"Are you sure?"

"I was just gonna ask you about some weird shit that went on, but it's so funny that you'd think I was losing my mind...so never mind. Not important." Emma knew it was off the wall, but she didn't want her mom worrying about her any more than she already did.

"Weird stuff?" she asked skeptically.

"Yeah, but it's not a big deal. I've got it under control," Emma assured her.

"Well, if you wanna talk, I'm here." That was the truth. Emma never felt like she had to keep a secret from her mom.

Emma's phone beeped, signaling another incoming call. "Mom, I've got another call. I'll talk to you later. Love ya, bye!" Switching lines, Emma picked up the other phone call. "Hello?"

"Hey, I'm just seeing when you'll be here," Kyle answered.

"I thought lunch wasn't 'til one!" Emma cried, looking over at her clock. It was only eight.

"It is, but there's a guy in my office who wants to meet you."

"Umm…you have a hard time telling me if the pizza guy is hot, but now you're playing matchmaker?" Emma teased, rolling her eyes, "Kyle, I'm worried about you."

"I'm not playing matchmaker, I've talked about you before, and he just broke up with his girlfriend and was asking about you."

Emma rolled her eyes again. "What's his name?" she asked curiously.

"Damon."

"Hmm…I dunno." Emma was skeptical on the whole 'fix up' situation.

"Well, hurry up and get here!" Kyle snapped.

"You're the pushiest person ever! I'll be there a little early," Emma promised.

"See ya."

"Bye," Emma sighed, hanging up the phone. She sat on the edge of her bed, sipping her coffee. Since it was only eight fifteen, she had plenty of time to chill out and relax before getting ready.

Switching on her TV, she flipped through the ridiculous junk they called daytime television. The crap that people watched honestly made her question her sanity, and she began to wonder how she was still zoned in on it. She quickly snapped out of it, throwing the remote back onto the bed. "I'm so bored," Emma grumbled.

After moments of looking around her room for something to do, she finally decided to start getting ready. If she was going to make a good impression for Kyle and his boss, she needed to put a bit more effort into herself. Since she had the extra time, a long, hot shower was called for.

***

Standing under the hot water for twenty minutes was probably the best thing Emma had done for herself in a while. She still had yet to figure out what she was going to wear to lunch. Kyle didn't say no to jeans, so she grabbed her skinny jeans from the hanger and a silver and white striped shirt. Her black, high-heeled ankle boots would be the dressed-up part.

After she finished checking herself in the mirror, she quickly called for a taxi. Thankfully, the dispatcher said one would be at her place in five minutes. Wrapping a scarf around her neck, she grabbed her coat and purse and walked into the living room. Kyle had left a twenty on the counter for the cab ride down. He could be so demanding, but so sweet at the same time. Emma snatched the cash and headed toward the door.

As she reached the bottom of the stairs, she expected to see a cab waiting for her, but instead, Micah was standing outside in front of his SUV.

"You look beautiful," he said, smiling as he walked up to her.

"Hi! Thank you," Emma responded, blushing. The man could tell her that a balloon was red and make her melt.

"I wanted to come by and say hi. The phone is not a great way to ask a woman out on a date," he stated before kissing her on the cheek.

"I…uh…" Emma began to stutter.

"So, would you happen to be free tonight? I'm having a grand opening and I'd like you to join me."

"*Your* grand opening?" Emma asked, puzzled.

"Yeah, for my club, Ominous."

She stood there a little in shock "Well, I guess I could go," she said coolly. Who was she kidding? She definitely wanted to go with him.

"All right, I'll be here at ten." He pulled her in closer and placed another light kiss on her cheek. She felt like she had lost all of her ability to speak, so she just nodded.

He turned and got back into his Lexus just as the taxi pulled up to the curb. Emma just stood there, watching him drive away.

"Hey, lady, did you call for a cab?" the driver asked impatiently.

"I'm sorry, yes. Can you take me to Ninth and Broadway?" she asked, sliding into the backseat. During the entire drive, she couldn't take her mind off of the incredibly dirty things she wanted to do to Micah. Unfortunately, it was a short drive and her amazing fantasy was interrupted by the rude cab driver.

"That'll be ten fifty," the driver informed her when they arrived. He pulled up a block away from Kyle's building. Emma huffed. He could've at least dropped her in front of the building. She handed him the twenty and waited for her change. Handing him three bucks for a tip, she exited the car. It was only an extra thirty feet away, but the cold air made it feel unbearable. As she walked to Kyle's building, she was stuffing her wallet back into her purse when an older man collided with her.

"I'm so sorry!" Emma quickly apologized, placing a hand on his arm. She felt a weird sensation on the tips of her fingers. He didn't respond, but his dark eyes locked onto hers. Emma hated downtown, people seemed so much weirder. "Are you okay?" she asked.

"I'm fine," he said coldly, running his hand through his salt and pepper hair.

"Well...take it easy," she told him, feeling rather awkward as he continued to stare. Making sure she still had her purse, she walked past him and headed into Kyle's office. It almost felt like she knew the older man from somewhere. It was going to drive her crazy thinking of how and where she knew him from. Maybe he was just a customer from the coffee shop.

Walking past the front desk, Emma wandered toward a group of desks that reminded her of an episode of *The Office*, all of them pushed together in the middle of the room. "Em!" Kyle shouted, snapping her back to reality. She waved to him, walking back to his desk. As she approached, there was a good-looking guy standing at his desk.

Please, dear God, let that be Damon, Emma prayed to herself. "Emma Blackwood, this is Damon Ryder," Kyle introduced.

"Hi," she said bashfully, shaking his hand. Was every man suddenly gorgeous?

"Pleased to meet you, Emma. Kyle talks about you. A lot. We were actually all surprised when he said that you guys weren't together," he chuckled. His brown hair was perfectly styled back and God, he had incredible blue eyes. This man screamed sex god.

"It's nice to meet you too, Damon, but have you actually met Kyle? Could you see anyone settling down with *him*?" Emma laughed, nudging Kyle in the arm.

"So, you're paying for your own lunch?" Kyle joked.

"Har-har, don't be a crybaby. I'm pretty sure I'm doing *you* the favor, Mr. Anderson." Emma poked Kyle in the arm. She could feel Damon's eyes locked onto her.

"Ah, fuck. All right. Well, I think we'll head out in a minute," Kyle stated, putting some papers in his desk drawer.

"Are you going with us, Damon?" Emma asked. She could see that he had to quickly look away, trying to make it not so obvious that he was watching her.

"Not today, I'm not on Phil's team, but I'm sure we can all meet up for drinks one night soon though," he suggested as he winked at her.

"That'll be fun," she agreed, smiling. Was she flirting now?

"Well, Emma, I need to get back to work. It was very nice to meet you." Damon playfully slugged Kyle as he started to walk away.

"Yes. It was very nice to meet you too, Damon." Emma smiled, watching him as he walked to his desk on the other side of the room.

"You can stop drooling now," Kyle joked.

"Shut up! You're the one who wanted to introduce us," she huffed, smacking his arm.

"I didn't think you'd throw yourself at him. Anyway, you hungry?" Kyle stood up from his desk, locking his computer.

"Starving! I only had coffee this morning."

"Well, lemme go grab everyone else and we can make our way out to lunch." Kyle started to walk to the front of the office, but Emma grabbed his sleeve before he could leave.

"Wait, I'm the last one to arrive?" she panicked.

"Well, Phil's wife works as the receptionist and then there are only two other people going and they're dating."

"I'm seeing a trend of dating someone in the office. Who are you after?" Emma wiggled her eyebrows, looking around the office.

"Uh, no one," he said, shaking his head.

"Damon is pretty hot," she joked, laughing.

"Very funny. Let's go." Kyle nudged her with his elbow. He grabbed his blazer that was on the back of his chair and slipped it on before making their way out of the office.

Chapter Six

As far as business lunches went, this was pretty normal. They were chatting about work, what each of them were doing for the holidays, and while everyone was really nice, Emma kind of felt a little out of place. However, Kyle had tried to keep her included as much as possible. As everyone began to finish up eating and thanked their boss for paying, Kyle asked Phil if he could head out a bit early to take Emma home. His boss was more than happy to let him.

"Did you have fun at lunch?" Kyle asked Emma as they pulled away from the restaurant.

"Yeah, it was nice. So, I'm going out tonight," she declared excitedly.

"With Morton?" Kyle joked.

"It's Micah, you ass. And, yes."

"Close enough. Where are you kids going?" Kyle questioned.

Emma shrugged her shoulders. "Some new club that's opening. Apparently he owns it."

"Ominous," Kyle stated.

"It's a night club, how weird could that be?" Emma asked, confused.

"No, first, *ominous* doesn't really mean weird. Secondly, that's the club's name."

"Oh. How do you know?"

"Damon is actually doing a review on them. He'll be there too."

"Seriously? Huh." She started to blush.

"Huh?" Kyle gave her a confused look.

"Yeah, just...two hot men at the same time?" Emma wiggled her eyebrows at Kyle and began to snicker.

"You've been hanging out with me for too long." Kyle lightly pushed Emma.

They laughed as Kyle pulled into the garage. Maybe she had been hanging with Kyle too long, especially if she had a brief fantasy of both Micah and Damon...at the same time.

"Oh, hey, can I use your car?" she asked before stepping out.

"My car? For what?" Kyle loved his car, he was rather protective of his 'baby.'

"Well, I don't really have anything to wear tonight. Since I'm not really a dressy kinda chick and a dress is necessary tonight, I need your car to go find something to wear!" Emma linked her hands together, begging Kyle for the keys.

Kyle reluctantly tossed her the keys. "Please, be careful."

"Just because I don't have a car doesn't mean that I don't know how to drive! I'm always careful."

"Yeah, *always careful*. Like the time you backed out of your mom's driveway and took off her side mirror on the side of the garage?" Emma remembered there was also a bottle of wine involved. Everyone had been drinking and Emma was volunteered to pull the car in. Unfortunately she put it in reverse rather than drive.

"It was an *accident*!" Emma shrieked.

"Umm, no one said that you did it on purpose. I'm just sayin' don't have any accidents with *my* car."

"I won't." She smiled widely. "Thank you!"

"Do you want any company?" Kyle offered.

"So you can drive? No, thanks! I'll be home in a bit." Emma climbed over to the driver's side and turned the engine back on. What Kyle didn't know was that Emma had driven his car a couple of times when he went to Vegas with a few of his buddies. She *loved* driving it.

She pulled out of the garage—mirrors still intact—and made her way to the mall. She had no idea what she was even looking for, but it had to be glamorous. She couldn't be on the arm of the sexy guy who owned the place, looking like she worked at a coffee shop. Which she did.

Speeding down the road, she began to blast the music and found herself snapping to a song she had yet to learn the lyrics to. After one loud snap, the light changed from red to green. "Purely coincidence," she said quietly.

Approaching a light that had just changed to red, she snapped her fingers again. It, too, changed right away. "Are you fucking kidding me? I can change lights now too!" Emma placed both of her hands on the steering wheel and avoided doing anything else with her hands for the rest of the drive.

***

Having searched four stores, trying on what seemed like hundreds of dresses, and annoyed at least five employees, Emma was slowly losing hope and beginning to think of the best excuse to cancel for the night. She needed to wash her hair for the third time…today…because if she didn't it got really…nope, not going to work. Micah was too hot to cancel on anyway. "Why can't I be like Cinderella and have a magical fairy come put a dress on me?" she muttered to herself.

Before she completely threw in the white flag and stuffed herself with ice cream, she wandered into one last store. "Can I help you find something?" She turned to see an attractive blonde standing behind her. The girl almost reminded her of Gwen Stefani—bleached blonde hair and very red lips.

"Yeah, I'm looking for something to wear tonight. I'm not sure what I want though."

"We have some great dresses back this way," she said, leading Emma toward the back of the store. Three racks full of evening dresses were waiting for her to try on. "If you need anything, I'm Katia. Just give me a holler, okay?"

"Thanks." Stepping into the fitting room, Emma began to try on several dresses. Reason number four hundred and eighty-one why she needed to have girlfriends: she needed girls' opinions on her outfits, even if they did tell her a lie. She needed *somebody*.

"Everything okay?" Katia asked, knocking on the door.

"Umm, can I ask you for your opinion?" Emma asked skeptically.

"Sure, come on out," Katia insisted. She had obviously had many women shoppers come in on their own. Emma didn't feel so bad asking for help.

She had slipped on a black, lacy number and opened the door. Katia's eyes slightly widened as she stepped out of the room. "Does this look okay?" Emma asked, giving a small twirl.

"It fits you just right! I think this dress is for you," Katia answered.

Half-tempted to do a little dance, Emma passed on looking like an idiot in front of a complete stranger. She smiled politely and closed the door to the fitting room. *Then* did a little dance. Carefully slipping it off of herself, she looked at the price tag. "Jesus Chri…"

"Everything okay?" Katia interrupted. Emma didn't realize that Katia was still in the fitting area.

"Oh, yeah. I…uh…just hit my elbow." The price of the dress was more than she was looking to spend. Ever. "There's not possibly a sale going on, is there?"

"All evening wear is forty percent off."

"Oh good!" It was still more than Emma was looking to spend, so she quickly put her clothes back on and walked out of the fitting room.

Approaching the checkout counter, a tall man was chatting up Katia. His voice rang familiar as she inched closer. He slowly turned toward her and she realized it was Micah.

"Hey, Emma," he said as if he was expecting her.

"Um. Hi? What are you doing here?" she asked, confused.

"I swung by your place earlier and Kyle said that I might find you here. Find anything good?" He inspected the dress on the hanger.

"Yeah, I found this dress. I wanted to be a little dressy tonight."

"I bet you'd look hot in anything you wore." He turned and faced Katia, handing her a credit card.

"What are you doing?" She gulped as he took the dress from her and handed it to Katia.

"What does it look like?" Micah smiled, taking his card back from Katia.

"It looks like you've lost your mind."

"Nope, still intact," he said, touching the top of his head. "I'm buying you this dress."

"Look, I'm not sure if I can accept this," she confessed.

"Emma, you're accompanying me to a press-filled, public event. It's the least that I can do," he purred, handing her the garment bag.

"I'd like to pay you back for this," Emma insisted.

"Consider it a thank you gift," Micah offered.

"No, seriously." Emma began to rummage through her purse for the cash she had in one of the pockets.

"I'm being serious. I told you, there will be a lot of press at this opening. I'm happy that I'm going to have you by my side. With that being said, I'm more than happy to help out. Are you hungry?"

"No, I'm still rather full from lunch. I could go for a soda though. My treat?" Emma smiled.

He chuckled, leading the way toward the food court. So far, he had purchased a dress for her and she'd only just found out what he did for a living. Beyond that, she really didn't know anything else about him. She bought them each a soda and took a seat at a table. "So, Micah…" Emma began.

"Yes?" Micah leaned in.

"Care to tell me a bit about yourself? I mean, I don't really know anything about you."

"Well, not much to tell. I moved around a lot, I went to college and majored in business. I decided I didn't want to have anyone telling me what to do, so I opened up a small bar back home; I liked it so much, I branched out. I moved here about a month ago, and here we are."

"Where is back home?" she inquired.

"New York."

"Oh yeah? I'm from Ipswich." She liked the idea that he was from the East Coast too.

"We're practically neighbors, then," he said, placing his hand on hers. The energy between their hands was enough to send off a spark.

"Sorry, I didn't mean to shock you!" Emma quickly apologized, pulling her hand back.

"Please, don't apologize." He leaned over the table, softly kissing her lips. This guy was something else. "Emma…" They were suddenly interrupted by his cell phone ringing in his jacket pocket. "I'm sorry, I need to take this." He excused himself from the table and went toward the entrance of the mall.

Sitting there, reflecting on how fast things were moving, Emma pulled out her phone and called up Kyle.

"House of Horny, you got the dough, we got the ho," Kyle answered.

"You're seriously a pig!" Emma laughed. Kyle had funny ways of answering the phone. Once he answered the phone acting as a mafia guy wanting to know where she wanted to dump a body. Emma often wondered about Kyle's sanity.

"So, you got the dough?" He laughed. "Did you find what you were looking for?"

"Yeah, I did. Oh, and thanks for telling Micah where I was…"

"What?" he asked.

"He said he came by our place and you told him I was at the mall."

"Uhh…I haven't seen him since the other night." Emma's stomach suddenly felt like it dropped.

"Huh. That's weird." If Kyle hadn't told Micah…she began to wonder how Micah knew where she was. "Anyway, I'm about done here. Want me to bring home some dinner?"

"I'm actually going out with Zoe, and then Damon got us some tickets to go to that club you're going to."

"Great! I won't feel so weird and not know anyone. Well, I'll just see you there, then?"

"Yep. Hey…" he began.

"What?" Emma asked as she watched Micah talk on his phone.

"Be careful, okay?" he begged.

"Yes, Daddy," Emma joked.

"You know, it's kinda hot when you call me that," Kyle chuckled.

"Shut up, I'll talk to you later!" She hung up the phone, shaking her head. As Micah walked back toward the table, she slipped her phone back into her purse. Watching him come toward her, it almost felt like they were the only two people in the entire food court.

"I need to head out," Micah began. "But I want to take you to dinner before the club. I'll pick you up at eight. Will that give you enough time to get ready?"

"It should be fine. What time is it now?" Emma asked. She looked down at her wrist and realized she forgot to put her watch on this morning.

"Close to five," Micah answered, looking at his phone.

"Geez! I've spent too long at the mall. I'm going to head home, then. Thank you for the dress, Micah," she said, standing up from the table and grabbing her bags.

"It was my pleasure." He pulled her chin up and kissed her lips once more. "Mmm, so sweet."

How was she supposed to respond to that? She felt her knees get weak, so she did what she did best. Smiled. Emma turned the opposite direction from Micah and made her way back to Kyle's car. Micah had some sort of power over her and she couldn't tell if she wanted it, or just couldn't fight it.

Chapter Seven

Kyle had already left by the time Emma arrived home. Zoe must've picked him up, especially since she still had his car. She found a note on the fridge, warning her that there better not be any sort of scratches on Hi Ho Silver when he got home. What grown man named his vehicle? Kyle, that's who. Emma never really understood it, but whatever.

She took a quick shower and made sure she shaved her legs. Who knew what would happen tonight? Not that she had any sort of high hopes, but one could never be too sure. She cut the tags off her dress and slipped it on, putting her robe on over the dress so she wouldn't get any makeup on it. She still had an hour until Micah arrived, so she stood in front of the mirror, pondering how to wear her hair. She only knew ponytails.

"Hey, Em? Kyle left..." Emma heard Zoe's voice screeching through the apartment. What the hell was she doing here?

"What?" Emma asked, poking her head out of her bedroom.

"Kyle left his phone here, so he sent me up to grab it. Is that what you're wearing?" Zoe looked Emma up and down, giving her a look of disapproval.

"No. This is a *robe*, Zoe," Emma snapped. Was she really that blonde?

"Oh, well, I guess we're going to be seeing you later?" Zoe smiled, smacking her gum.

"Yep. Can you do me a favor? Have Kyle text me when you give him his phone?" Emma asked in her nicest voice.

"If I remember. See ya." Zoe waved as she walked out the door, barely closing it.

Emma began to wonder why Kyle had to pick the dumbest skank out of them all. Emma shut the door completely, locking it. When she turned around, she found a thong with a kissy note to Kyle lying behind the couch. What kind of person did that? Emma wished Zoe could be a bit more likable. She really needed someone who knew about hair and makeup to help her out. "Back to the drawing board," she sighed, walking back to her bathroom.

After forty minutes of messing with the curling iron, Emma mastered loose, ringlet curls. She was pretty satisfied with the way it turned out. Micah was going to be there in less than a half hour and she still needed to put her makeup on, so she rushed through what she knew best. Emma heard her phone beep from her room.

Kyle: Hey, Zoe said to text you. What's up?

Wow, Zoe could remember things for more than

a minute. Emma quickly responded.

Emma: What time will you be at the club? I wanna meet you later.

She was suddenly a nervous wreck! Micah had so much sex appeal and felt so...powerful. Kyle quickly responded.

Kyle: Going for drinks and dinner now. Call you when we get there.

Setting her phone down on the bed with her purse, a buzz came from the front door. She straightened her dress and rushed to the door. Micah—dressed all in black—stood at the door, looking sexier than ever. "Don't you look sexy?" Micah greeted.

"Thanks," she responded, blushing. "You're looking pretty damn good yourself." Emma opened the door a bit wider, inviting him to come in.

"You ready? I reserved us a spot at Panzano's."

"Yeah, let me grab my coat." As she began to walk away, his hand softly grabbed her wrist, pulling her back against him.

"I'm going to kiss you. But I don't know if I can stop at just that," he whispered into her mouth. Emma felt her knees become weak as his lips gently touched hers. His hands combed through her hair, pulling her head back as his lips moved down her neck. "Emma..." Just the whisper of her name made her come undone.

"Micah?" Emma moaned.

"I'm going to wait until after this party," he stated firmly.

"What?" she asked, a little too loud. Emma's ego suddenly felt bruised.

Micah chuckled. "I know, but once we're alone in a room…" he kissed her neck once more, "…I'm not going to want to leave, and unfortunately, it's my grand opening and I should probably be there."

Goddamn it. Emma hated that answer and she wasn't happy about having to wait until after the party. She slightly nodded, turning away from him, and pretended to sulk as she walked to her room, grabbing her purse and coat from the desk. He was going to have to stop teasing her.

"All right, I'm all set," she announced, straightening her dress as she walked back down the hallway. Micah stood in the living room, looking at her intensely as his eyes turned a dark shade of gray.

"Ah, fuck it," Micah whispered, rushing toward her. Picking her up and carrying her through the room, he pressed his lips hard onto hers. Her legs wrapped tightly around his waist as her hands combed wildly through his hair. "How do you get this dress off?"

"Zipper is on the side," she breathed, sliding down him as he fumbled with the zipper. Micah quickly undressed himself as she stood patiently waiting. Watching him undress, after months of not being with anyone, made her blush. His naked body was incredibly toned in all the right spots and he was standing in *her* room.

"Lie down," he instructed.

76

Emma did as she was told, making her way to the head of the bed. Her heart was about to beat out of her chest as he stood beside her. He slowly wrapped his black tie around her wrists and then held them above her head. Holy shit, this was exactly like her dream!

He lay down beside her, staring deep into her eyes. "Spread your legs," he whispered. His hand glided up from her ankle toward her thigh and slowly spread her slickened folds, beginning to massage her clit. "You're so wet, I can't wait to be inside of you." He leaned in and kissed her neck, softly nibbling at her skin.

She tried to move her hands, but he pressed down on them. Being tied down was slightly terrifying, yet so erotic. He lifted himself up on top of her and thrust, hard. "Oh my God!" Emma screamed. As he began to push harder and faster, a sudden feeling of power and energy began to surge through her veins. She'd never felt anything like this in her life.

"Do you feel that?" Micah groaned into her ear. She nodded. At that moment, she wondered how he knew exactly what she was feeling.

"Keep going, this is amazing!" she screamed. Just as she let her entire body succumb to the greatest orgasm ever, the light on the desk burst. She'd never seen anything like it, except maybe in a movie. She couldn't explain how, but she knew something was different now.

***

Once they had cleaned up, they arrived at the restaurant forty minutes late. It was definitely worth it though. She'd thought for sure that the restaurant would have bumped their reservation, but the manager was more than willing to accommodate them. Apparently he and Micah had known each other from way back. The food was incredible. Lamb that melted on her tongue, scallops that were so flavorful, and crisp wine. Emma wanted to ask Micah about this 'feeling' that she was having, but she didn't want to possibly ruin the evening by sounding a little clingy, as Kyle would call it.

"Everything okay?" he asked, taking one last drink of his wine.

"Hmm? Yeah, just enjoying this delicious food. And you?" Emma lied.

"You've been quiet since we left your place." Micah grabbed her hand and began to rub it reassuringly.

"I don't mean to be. I…" Emma started.

"You don't really know, do you?" Micah asked, surprised.

"Know what?" She looked at him, puzzled. What could she possibly know that he would know?

"We'll talk later tonight. We should probably head to the club. You still okay with going?"

"Of course! My roommate, Kyle, should be there too." Emma smiled.

"Oh yeah?" he asked, intrigued at her announcement.

"Yeah, he works for the paper and his co-worker is covering your opening, so he invited him and his…umm…latest skank?"

78

Micah chuckled. "Well, I'll see to it that they all get VIP."

"That's very kind of you." Emma was really impressed with all of Micah's kindness.

"Shall we?" Micah asked, standing up.

"Yes." She stood up and he helped her with her coat.

As they walked out of the restaurant, a limo was waiting at the curb for them. "I figured that we would both be having a few drinks, so I wanted us to get home safely," he said, smiling as the driver opened the door.

"Wow, you're really pulling all the strings tonight, aren't you? Where is your car, though?" Emma joked, sliding into the backseat.

"Only the best," he said, smiling. "I had one of my bar managers take it to your place. I wanted us to be able to take the limo to the club." Before this evening, Emma had never been in a limousine. This was by far an evening she never expected or thought she may experience. She didn't know if she was going to be able to keep accepting all of these lavish treats. As they situated themselves into the limo, Micah poured her a glass of champagne. She was not one to be spoiled, even as an only child, but she was certainly enjoying it now.

"So, how did you come up with the name Ominous for the club?" Emma asked, taking a sip of the crisp champagne.

"I tend to like things a bit darker in nature and so it seemed fitting."

"Oh, I see. I kinda like it."

"You like the darker side of things, Emma?"

"I'm not sure," she said with a smile.

Finishing the last of their champagne, they pulled up to a building swarmed with cameras and people waiting to get in. The driver came around and opened the door just as the reporters ran to meet Micah. "Mr. Oliver! Can we get a moment?" one reporter shouted.

"Micah, who's the lady you're with tonight? How are you feeling about the turnout for this club?" another asked, waving a hand holding a pen and paper.

"Mr. Oliver, Mr. Oliver! Can you pose for a few pictures?" a man with a camera shouted, taking photographs anyway.

Wow, he was not only gorgeous, but well-known. "Emma, do you mind if we take a few pictures?" Micah asked.

"No, of course not," she replied nervously. Micah looked like he was definitely enjoying the attention of all of the reporters. He placed his arm around her and began to smile in the direction of all the flashes. Emma tried to keep her cheesy grin to a bare minimum.

They walked through the flashing lights and smiled in every direction. Standing behind the crowd, Emma spotted Kyle. She suddenly felt a bit more comfortable seeing his smile; she gave him a small wave and excused herself from Micah's embrace.

"Ms. Blackwood, how are you enjoying the attention?" a male voice asked.

Emma turned to see Damon standing behind her with a pad and pen in his hands, looking very suave in his white button-up shirt and black pants. "I'm having a great time, thank you. Have you met Micah yet?"

"Mr. Oliver? No, but I'm now hoping you'll introduce us."

"I'd love to." Emma walked over to Micah, pulling on his hand to grab his attention. "Micah, this is Damon Ryder, he works with Kyle at the paper. Mind helping him out?"

"Of course not. Damon, was it?" They shook hands while she excused herself to see Kyle. Emma ran up to Kyle excitedly.

"Hey! I'm so glad that you're here now. I feel so weird being in front of those cameras!" She sighed, hugging him.

"You look beautiful," he said as he pulled away.

"Thanks, Kyle. Where's Zoe?" Emma asked, looking around the crowd.

"She had to run back to the car, she left her chap gloss or gloss stick, whatever the fuck it's called." Kyle rolled his eyes as he motioned putting something on his lips.

"Lip gloss?" Emma giggled.

"Yeah, that's it," he chuckled.

"Micah said that he's gonna get you guys VIP status!" She smiled, playfully smacking his arm.

"Sweet. I just need a drink, so I don't care what status I'm at." Kyle's ideal nightclub was one that you could wear jeans and a nice shirt in. Wearing something more was too upscale. He did, however, look great in his dress pants and button-down shirt.

"Sure you do. Either way, should we head in?" Emma asked, looking around for Micah.

"Yeah, go grab loverboy and we'll get you chocolate wasted," Kyle joked, pushing Emma.

"You're an idiot," she laughed, walking away. The look on Micah's face as he spoke with Damon worried her and she was happy to interrupt. "Everything okay?"

"Yes, we're fine," Damon snapped.

"Unfortunately, Mr. Ryder is not going to be able to join us this evening," Micah said sternly.

Both of them had yet to break eye contact. They were obviously having a heated discussion before she interrupted. Micah broke the stare, grabbing Emma's hand and heading toward the entrance.

"Emma, wait!" Damon shouted, following her. She turned back to see him and saw his fists were clenched, but as her hand flew back to stop Damon from coming closer, a feeling like an electric shock burst from her fingertips and knocked Damon to the ground.

"What the hell was that?" Emma screamed as Micah pulled her toward the club. "Micah! You saw that, right? I need to see if he's okay!"

"He'll be fine. He tripped. Let's get you a drink," he said, pulling her through the entrance.

"Are you sure? I should go back!" she argued. Emma had so many questions running through her mind. She was so confused, she could've sworn that she did something to Damon. How did one trip backwards?

"No, come on," Micah insisted.

As they walked toward the bar, Emma sighed, knowing he wasn't going to let her go back. She felt really weird that she just knocked a guy down without even touching him, and Micah didn't even question it. Kyle and Zoe were already ordering their drinks. Zoe was hanging all over him, laughing and kissing up and down his neck. As Micah and Emma approached, Zoe stopped and smiled at Micah. An older gentleman with blond hair was working behind the bar, handing out drinks. He stopped serving others and walked toward the end of the bar to greet Micah. "Felix, this lovely lady and her friends are my guests. Please get them anything they want," Micah instructed the bartender. Felix only replied with a nod.

"Em, whatcha want?" Kyle asked.

"I'll have a beer," Emma ordered.

"Kyle, honey, will you get me a Cosmo?" Zoe asked, kissing him on the neck.

"Zoe, may I take your jacket?" Micah asked, taking her coat.

"Please! Such a gentleman." Zoe batted her eyelashes.

Kyle and Emma rolled their eyes as Zoe danced over to Micah, trying to seductively remove her coat. She followed Micah toward the coat check, while Kyle and Emma stayed behind for their drinks.

"She really is something else, huh?" Kyle asked, taking a drink of his beer.

"She's what the kids on the street call a gold digger." Emma laughed.

"Nah, she's just…not that bright. But, Em, if I tell ya something, promise not to get bent out of shape?"

"Oh my God, you procreated with her!" Emma

sneered.

"Fuck, no! But…I'm thinking of keeping things exclusive with her."

"Why?" Emma gave Kyle a look of disgust. He just told her that she wasn't that bright, why would he want to keep things exclusive?

"Why? 'Cause I like her…"

"She was all flirty with Micah a minute ago, though," Emma snapped.

"Well, it's not really official yet. I was gonna talk to her about it tonight."

Emma sighed. "You really sure about this? I mean Tiana was just a girlfriend."

"Not really. She *said* she was. I really like Zoe."

"Well, you do seem to have her over more than any other girl, so it was pretty obvious it was going to happen."

"Was it really that obvious?" Kyle asked.

"Pretty much, but as long as you're happy. I mean if you're *really* happy…I'll be happy for you." Emma smiled genuinely at Kyle.

"Thanks, Em. You really are my best friend. So, what about this guy, you think that he's boyfriend material?"

"I'm not sure what this is, but there *is* something going on." She smiled, watching Micah and Zoe walk back toward them. Zoe had since let go of Micah, which made Emma a little happier. Zoe wasn't able to suck this guy in. Or better yet, off. Emma chuckled to herself.

"Care to dance?" Micah asked, holding out his hand. Emma set her beer on the bar and eagerly grabbed his hand.

"See you guys out there?" she asked, walking away. Kyle waved, smiling.

Micah led Emma to a dark dance floor, where several other couples had already started to dance along with the music. Katy Perry's "Dark Horse" came over the speakers, and Micah pulled her closer. "So, have you figured it out?" he asked, kissing her ear.

"Figured what out?" she asked, confused.

"What I was going to talk to you about?" His hand rubbed up and down her back, sending goose bumps down her arms. His fingers made her feel so good.

"I'm kinda still in awe about what's happened this entire night. Is this all connected?"

"It is. Emma, I'm the same," Micah confessed.

"Wait, what?" Emma pushed him away, her heart stopped. The same? The same what?

"It's hard to explain, but with some help, I think that we'll be amazing together."

"Help with what?" Emma demanded.

"With the power that you have, I think you have the potential to be a very powerful person."

"Really? But I don't even know what this is!" Emma was now more confused than ever. She had powers?

"You'll soon learn, but I think that you are much stronger than you know." He kissed up and down her neck as his hands explored her body. Their bodies moved slowly to the music. It was as if they were the only ones in the club. His arms reached behind her, she held onto the back of his head as his hand slipped underneath her dress. It was like he didn't care that there could be several eyes watching. "I can't wait to get you back out of this dress," he whispered in her ear. Every part of her wanted to feel more of him, even if it were on the dance floor.

"Hey, Emma?" Emma heard Zoe's voice come up behind them. She pulled away from Micah to see Zoe holding onto Kyle.

"Is he okay?" Emma asked, looking at Kyle in a panic. His face was so white, it looked as if he had seen a ghost.

"I think he might have some food poisoning. He was drinking his beer and then he had to run to the bathroom. He said he's not feeling well."

Kyle really didn't look good at all. "Here, let me grab my things! We should probably get him to the ER," Emma insisted. She had never seen Kyle look like this, even after a frat party their sophomore year.

"No, I'm fine. I'm just gonna go home," Kyle groaned.

"Kyle, you look like hell! I think you need help!" Emma cried.

"Nah, just probably some bad Mexican," Kyle said, grabbing his stomach.

"I'm gonna take him home. If I need your help, can I call you?" Zoe asked.

"Yeah, of course. I should be home a little later, but my phone is on." Emma reached in her purse, making sure her phone was on.

"Thanks, Emma. Have fun," Zoe said, walking out with Kyle.

"Wow, Kyle has always had a steel stomach.

He's looking pretty bad," Emma said, turning to face Micah.

"Yeah, he looked pretty bad. Did you want to leave?" he asked, motioning at the exit.

"No, I mean, I should, but I think that he's gonna be fine. Zoe said she'd call if they were gonna go to the hospital."

"All right. Well, would you like a drink? Dance?" Micah asked, caressing her arm.

"Both." Emma smiled. She was worried about Kyle, but she didn't want to miss out on learning more from Micah.

Chapter Eight

Micah and Emma spent the rest of the evening dancing and drinking. Micah needed to stay until the place was completely empty. Although Emma was tired, it didn't bother her to stay because it meant she had more time to spend with Micah. After he'd told her that he was able to do the same sort of 'things' she was able to, she didn't know if she should believe him. Emma did feel a little better about the situation, but this was all still so new to her. She felt as if she was living in some sort of messed up dream. She had always been 'normal,' and yet, here she was, doing these 'things.'

As Micah locked up the club, Emma climbed into the limo to warm up and watched him speak to one of the bar's managers. Even with a stern look on his face, he looked sexy. Suddenly, the other door of the limo opened and a masked man, holding a knife, slid into the backseat with her.

"Don't say a fucking word, just give me your purse and any jewelry," he said, gritting his teeth to mask his voice. He quietly closed the door so the overhead light would stay off.

"O-okay, b-but please d-don't hurt me," Emma stuttered, starting to cry. Of course, the privacy window had to be up.

"Bitch, I said don't say a fucking word! I will cut the shit outta you!" he threatened. Emma's heart was racing.

As she reached down, feeling for her handbag on the dark floor, she felt the same sort of current flow through her as when Damon had rushed toward her. If she was going to use it, or at least try, now was her chance. She threw her hand toward the guy and he went flying back against the door, dropping the knife.

"What the fuck?" he exhaled. Emma was relieved to see the knife finally out of his hands.

"I think it's best that you get the fuck outta the car," she said, trying to remain calm. Every part of her wanted to jump up with excitement. He quickly opened the door and took off running. Micah suddenly opened her door, causing her to jump.

"What the hell was that?" he asked, watching the guy run from the car.

"He tried to rob me!" Emma shrieked.

"Are you okay?" Micah pulled her close to his body, combing his fingers through her hair.

"Yeah…actually, I feel great. I just had a guy pull a knife out and threaten me, but I somehow managed…Micah, what the hell is going on? I've never been able to do this in my life and now, I'm pushing men around without even touching them! I didn't know what was going on, but I was excited," she said in what sounded like one breath.

"Let's get you home."

Nodding, Emma pushed herself away from him and sat back into the seat. She couldn't tell if it was adrenaline pumping through her body, or if she actually felt more powerful. Either way, it was a great way to end the night. Micah rolled down the privacy window, instructing the driver to her place.

"What about your car?"

"I can get it in the morning."

"I hate to be forward, but are you staying with me tonight?"

"You're not being forward, but yes, I planned on it." He smiled, softly caressing the back of her neck. The anticipation of arriving at her place was killing her. She was going to have this man twice in one night.

As the driver pulled up to Emma's building, Micah motioned for him to stay in the car. He opened the door, holding out his hand to take hers, and escorted her out of the car. She took his hand before lacing her arm through his, walking toward the entrance of the building. Unlocking the front door, Emma could hear Zoe laughing from inside. Her laugh was like the sound of a monkey going crazy.

"Kyle?" Emma shouted.

"In the living room, Em."

"How you feeling?" Emma asked, setting her stuff on the table. Micah walked quietly behind her.

"Better, thanks. It was weird, I was drinking my beer and I felt a little…" Kyle stopped as he saw Micah walk into the room. "Hey, man. Sorry to have left your party early," Kyle said, sitting up on the couch.

"Don't apologize," Micah said, holding his hand up.

"Well, I'm glad that you're better!" Emma chimed in. Kyle did look one hundred percent better.

What a fast bout of food poisoning.

"Me too. I don't do well with puke," Zoe added.

"Ew, did you puke anywhere?" Emma looked around the place for signs of damage.

"No, just at the club. Once we got home I started to feel a bit better."

"I'm glad," Emma replied, patting Kyle on the arm. There was a moment of awkward silence between the four of them. "Well, I think we're gonna go…"

"You guys have fun. We're gonna turn in too. I've gotta be up early for work," Kyle declared, smiling at Emma like an idiot.

"Thank you both for coming, even if it was for a short time. If you want to try again, let me know and I'll get you in," Micah said, placing his hand on Emma's lower back.

"Thank you!" Zoe exclaimed.

"Night, guys," Emma said, pulling Micah toward her room. "Can I get you anything?" she asked him, closing the door.

"I'm fine for right now."

Emma took a seat on the bed, kicking off her shoes. She was relieved to take the heels off. "So, can I ask you something?"

"First, I need to get this dress off you and get you into bed," Micah stated. She blushed as he came toward her. His eyes became darker before he leaned in and kissed her shoulder. Standing her up, he slowly unzipped her dress. He kissed her shoulders, pushing her back onto the bed. "I'm going to *show* you what you probably want to ask."

"Oh my God, can you read minds?" She sat down on the edge of the bed in her bra and underwear.

"No, I can't read minds, entirely. I can see a 'vision' of what they are thinking. I can also 'sense' when someone is near."

"How do you mean?" she asked curiously. This was all so new to her, so she couldn't even believe she was having this sort of conversation.

"Which part?" he asked.

"Let's start with the vision part."

"That one is hard to explain. I can shake hands with someone and see what they are thinking about. I can't really read their minds, but I get glimpses of a thought or memory."

"Okay, now what about the sensing? Can you sense, like, if Kyle is coming down the hall?"

"No, I can't sense if Kyle is coming. I can sense the power of others and when someone with power comes near."

"So, wait, you knew I had powers?" she asked, trying to comprehend all that was being said to her.

"I wasn't sure, but I could sense you were special." He smiled.

"What else can you do?" she asked eagerly. He walked up to Emma and pushed her back, laying her on the bed, when the lights suddenly went out and the candles on her dresser began to flicker. "That is so cool!"

The candles slowly dimmed as he approached the side of the bed. Emma could feel his breath on her shoulder. "I'm not sure you're ready for the rest," he whispered.

"Try me," she whispered into his ear, nibbling on his lobe.

"Lie still." He stood up and walked to the end of the bed. She wasn't sure whether to feel scared or turned on. She could only see the outline of his body, but suddenly felt as if his arms were underneath her, lifting her off the bed.

"Micah?" Her voice trembled.

"Shh." Emma looked around to see where he was, but he wasn't at the foot of the bed. "Are you scared?"

"Surprisingly, no. Where are you?"

"Right here," he whispered, standing next to her. "I'm going to put you down." Her body began to lower; even though she was only inches off the bed, she felt like she was so much higher. The candles began to flicker again and Micah was lying on her bed underneath her. He wrapped his arms around her, pulling her onto him. One hand cupped her breast as the other made its way between her legs.

"This is all real?" Emma asked, looking down at him.

"Yes, Emma, this is all real," he groaned as she began to rock back and forth. She ripped open his shirt, the buttons flying everywhere. Her nails dug into his chest, scratching down his abdomen.

"Then let me feel everything. You said you wanted me to try the dark, and I want to feel the dark side of you." He grabbed her waist, pulling her off him as he rolled on top of her. Emma softly gasped.

"I want to bring you the darkness. Just let me in, something is holding you back. I'm not sure you're fully ready."

"How do I let go?" Emma moaned.

"It's not something I can tell you. You have to just let go," Micah instructed.

"But I still want to feel *you*," she begged. Every part of her wanted him more than ever.

"Don't worry, I'm going to give you *all* of me." He leaned in and kissed her. Hard. He tasted amazing. As their lips became inseparable, the candles began to flicker brightly.

Emma was giving the man all of her and she had to let go more? What more could she possibly do?

"I'll let go," she whispered.

***

The sun began to shine through Emma's window, warming her face. She rolled over to find that Micah had left at some point. Looking at the floor, she didn't see his clothes, but the buttons from his shirt were still scattered around the room. It made her smile at the memory of last night.

"Em, you up?" Kyle asked from behind the closed door.

She pulled the blankets closer to her chin. "Yeah, c'mon in." Kyle opened the door, covering his eyes. "It's okay, I'm dressed," she laughed. She didn't remember exactly when she had put on her tank and shorts, but she was clothed.

"Well, after last night, I didn't think you'd have the energy to put on any clothes," he joked, pulling his hand away from his eyes.

"What do you mean?" she asked, sitting up.

"I'm sure that everyone in the building heard you and Mr. Stamina." Kyle started making a humping movement and smacking his hand.

"Were we really that loud?" She gasped, covering her mouth.

"I think I had an orgasm just listening to you."

"That's gross." She made a disgusted face. "I'm sorry. I didn't think we were loud!"

"All good. I'm just gonna have to get Zoe to go louder next time." Kyle pulled at his chin as if he was coming up with some deviant plan.

"Uh, no thanks!" She gagged. "So, what's up?"

"Just heading into work. Hey, can I run something by you?" Kyle hesitantly asked.

"Sure!"

"You don't think that...I don't know, that something was slipped into my drink at the bar? I mean, did you see anything?" he asked, sitting on the edge of her bed.

"You think someone slipped you something?" Emma asked, surprised.

"Em, it was weird. I was drinking my beer and as Micah came to take you onto the dance floor, I suddenly felt really fucked up. I don't remember much after that. Zoe said I puked a lot and then we left."

"Do you remember when you got home?"

"That's the thing, the second we got home, I felt

fine. I wasn't sure why we were even home!" Kyle stood up, rubbing his head.

"That's really weird!"

"Yeah. So, I'm just gonna ask, do you think that Micah would have any reason to fuck with my drink?" Kyle asked in an accusatory tone.

"Kyle, you think that Micah did that to you?" Emma began to feel irritated. How in the world could he think that Micah would've done something like this?

"No, Em, don't get upset. I'm just asking," he said, sitting back on the bed. He tried to reach for her hands.

"It sounds more like you're accusing!" she shouted, pulling her hands away from him.

"Look, I didn't mean to upset you. I was just curious if you thought he could've done it."

"No," she snapped.

"Well, I'm heading out, will you be home later?" he asked, standing up, walking toward her door.

"Yeah, probably. I don't have work today, so I think I'm just gonna hang out here." Emma tried to hide the tears that were starting to build up. She was hurt that her best friend, the one who she really hoped would be supportive of any relationship she was in, was accusing Micah of drugging him.

"Zoe has some sort of family thing, so I'll bring home some dinner?" Kyle suggested.

"That'd be nice." She smiled.

"See ya, chick." Kyle waved, walking out of her room.

"Bye. Hey, Kyle," she hollered as he started to close her door.

"Yeah?" He opened the door, poking his head back in.

"I...I'm sorry," Emma stuttered.

"Don't be. I shouldn't have asked. I'll see ya later." He shut the door and she felt incredibly annoyed. Why would he even ask if he didn't think that it had happened?

"Okay," she whispered to herself. She could hear the front door slam shut as she lay back down onto her pillow. She didn't want to even think that Micah would do something like that. Out of the corner of her eye, Emma noticed a blood-red box on top of her desk. She hurried over, grabbing the box, and returned back to bed. Untying the black ribbon, she pulled out a beautiful black crystal tennis bracelet. It had two black crystal roses surrounded by black crystals. A note was tucked inside.

Dearest Emma, last night was magical. Someone as special as you deserves something special.

As she slipped on the bracelet, chills ran down her spine. It was like the bracelet empowered her. She'd never felt so...strong. She didn't know what this feeling was, but it was almost electrical. As she admired the bracelet, her phone started to ring on her nightstand.

"Good morning," Micah greeted before she could say anything. "Did you find your gift?"

"I did, thank you. It's beautiful. Where did you get it?" Emma asked, looking at her wrist.

"At a little shop called La Bella Morte. The owner, Ying, and I go way back. You'd like her, she's very talented at what she does."

"Creating beautiful jewelry?" Emma asked, hoping that it wasn't something more sexual.

"Among other things."

"You sound so sexy on the phone," she breathed.

"You're sexy altogether."

She blushed. Emma wanted so much more of him and couldn't wait until the next time. "When did you leave?"

"Early this morning. I needed to take care of some things." He stopped and talked to someone in the background for a moment, but quickly came back to her. "Get up and dressed, I'll be there in thirty."

"Where are we going?" Emma asked excitedly.

"I want to show you something. Get ready," Micah instructed.

"Okay." He hung up and Emma quickly jumped out of bed and felt a sharp pain overwhelm her, causing her to fold over. Something didn't feel right. She sat on the bed for a moment to let the pain pass. She felt a little weaker. "What the hell?" she whispered. Pushing herself off the bed, she slowly made her way toward the bathroom. The pain had finally receded and she went back to getting ready.

Chapter Nine

True to his word, Micah arrived at her apartment within thirty minutes. Rather than calling her to let her know that he had arrived, he walked all the way up to her apartment to get her. As they drove to the surprise, he still refused to tell her where they were going, and the excitement was eating her alive. Emma, fidgeting with the bracelet, looked out the window to see if anything was familiar in the area.

They were in the car for at least twenty minutes and she didn't recognize anything as they pulled up to a small building. "Where are we?" Emma whispered, looking around the neighborhood.

"After I told you about Ying, I thought what better time than now to introduce you to her."

Emma smiled as she opened the door, walking up the little walkway. Micah followed close behind her as they entered the building. She had a strange feeling that she had been here once before, which was a little weird because she'd never seen or heard of the place before Micah mentioned it.

"Micah, darling, back so soon?" A gorgeous

young woman greeted him with a smile.

"I wanted you to meet..." Micah began.

"Emma, it's nice to meet you," she interrupted. "I'm Ying."

"Oh, you made the bracelet! Thank you!" Emma exclaimed, holding her hand out to shake Ying's hand.

"You're very welcome." Ying grabbed Emma's hand tightly and closed her eyes briefly. "Micah, you picked a strong one."

"She's very strong," he agreed.

"I'm sorry, 'strong'?" Emma asked, confused.

"Ying can also sense powers. She is also capable..." Micah started.

"So, I'm strong in powers? What does that mean?" Emma interrupted.

"Yes, Emma. Your powers are very strong," Ying said before turning toward Micah. "Micah, can I speak to you in private for a moment?"

"Emma, do you mind? I'll only be a minute." Micah kissed her cheek, squeezing her hand as she shook her head. Taking this as an opportunity, Emma decided to look at the other jewelry.

Micah followed Ying down a narrow hallway into another room and shut the door. Emma began to browse the necklaces hanging from antique jewelry hangers. Everything was neatly put together with Shakespearean quotes around the room.

When shall we three meet again. In thunder, lightning, or in rain?

By the pricking of my thumbs. Something wicked

this way comes.

Emma could hear Micah starting to shout, but she couldn't hear exactly what he was saying because his voice sounded muffled. Suddenly, the door flew open and Micah stormed toward her. "Emma, let's head out," he huffed.

"Everything okay?" she asked, looking back to try to say her goodbyes to Ying, but didn't see her as they left the building. Micah pulled her to his car, opened the door, and helped her into the seat.

"Yeah, she's a little busy," he said, closing the door and running to the driver's side.

"Micah, what's going on?" Emma demanded as he started the car. "What did she mean that I'm really strong? I've only learned about these 'powers' recently."

"Emma...we'll talk about this later. How about something to eat?" Micah sighed, driving down the road. She nodded, feeling lost.

They pulled into a local diner that served breakfast all day. Emma sat in her seat, not knowing which emotion was overwhelming her more, confusion or anger. "Micah..."

"Let's go eat," he insisted.

"I...I don't want to eat right now. I want answers!" she shouted, watching Micah step out of the car and walk around to her side. He opened the door and helped her out, but before they went anywhere, he pulled her against him. As his warm lips pressed against hers, she felt some sort of magnetic power between the two of them.

"Emma, can you feel that?" he whispered into

her ear, tightly gripping her arms.

"Yes," she whispered. "What is it?" Nervous butterflies swarmed her stomach.

"I'm not sure. I've never felt it before."

"Is that good?"

"I hope so." He smiled as he looked at her intensely. "I'm going to take you to my place instead. Get in." Micah kissed her once more before helping her back into the car. She didn't want to question him anymore.

They were silent during the entire drive to his place. There was a different feeling between them, the feeling she had when they first met—the goosebumps, the chills, they were no longer there. This was so much greater. Was she beginning to feel the 'dark' he wanted her to feel? They pulled up to a building that looked like an old warehouse. Emma looked at him skeptically as he opened his door and came around the other side.

"Is this your place?" she asked, inspecting the building.

"Yes, the loft on the fifth floor. It's mine."

"I'm   sorry,   but   your   neighborhood looks…scary."

"I can assure you, it's fine."

Emma nodded as she followed him up toward the entrance of the building. The elevator looked like it was going to break down at any minute. Most of the windows along the entryway were broken and it was as cold inside as it was outside. The elevator door closed behind them and they rode up to the fifth floor. As the doors opened, they walked into a hallway with only two doors. Going to the door on the left, he unlocked the large steel door and guided her into an extravagant loft. Emma made a mental note not to judge a building by its exterior again.

Beautiful artwork hung on his walls and a king-sized bed was set up against a huge window, overlooking the Denver skyline. Black and red seemed to be all around his place, creating a darkened look. It made the room feel very exotic. He definitely seemed to like things dark. As Emma looked at some of the artwork, Micah walked up behind her and took her coat.

The artwork was not necessarily of any subject, but dark colors splashed upon an easel. Yet, it all still intrigued her. Micah set her coat on a chair near the front door and returned to her, his lips meeting her shoulder. "Can I get you anything?" he asked, lifting her sweater up over her head.

She shook her head, allowing her cami to follow the sweater to the floor. Standing in just her jeans and bra, he looked her up and down. "I want to try something," Emma said, smiling. She wanted to see if all this new feeling she had affected any of her newly found powers.

"Okay?" He looked at her skeptically as she walked him over to one side of the room. Emma watched him cross his arms as he stood in front of her. She closed her eyes. Stepping back from him, Emma wanted to see if she was anywhere near able to do what he did to her last night. She wanted to see if she could lift him and take him to the bed. "What do you want to do?"

"Shh, I'm concentrating," Emma said, peeking out one eye.

"Em…" he stopped. She felt that energy hitting her hands, the same feeling she'd had at the club. Emma imagined lifting Micah up onto the bed, laying him down on the pillow.

"You did it!" he shouted from the bed.

Her eyes quickly opened and she jumped up and down, clapping. "Oh shit! I did!" She ran over to the bed and threw herself down next to him. Their lips met once again. "Micah, I need to feel you inside me," she moaned into his mouth.

He wasted no time and ripped the rest of her clothing off her. Emma struggled to unbutton his pants, so she tried a flick of her wrist and his pants quickly unbuttoned. These powers were going to be extremely helpful after all.

Laying her down on the bed, he growled as he pulled her panties down her legs. Climbing over her, he gently spread her legs and kissed down her navel until his tongue began to tease her clit. Emma's back arched as he slowly inserted a finger inside of her. "Oh, Micah," she moaned.

"You like this, don't you?" he whispered into her ear.

"Mmm." Emma nodded, enjoying the feeling of him all around her.

"Tell me what you want, Emma. I want to hear you tell me," he instructed.

"Oh. My. God! I want…"

"That's it, you're so wet. Tell me," Micah demanded.

"I want to feel you inside of me!" she screamed.

He growled again as he removed his finger. Lining himself up to her entrance, he pushed deep inside of her. "Emma, give yourself to me."

"I'm all yours!"

As she lay in his arms, panting, she couldn't help but wonder—was this the start of something serious between them? She enjoyed being with him. The fact that he understood she had powers made Emma feel that she couldn't be with another man.

Her fingers traced up and down his chest to his navel as she tried to come up with a way to talk to him about what was on her mind. "Micah?"

"Hmm?" he breathed.

"I...is everything for you the same...I don't even know what I'm asking. I mean your powers...in relationships?" she nervously asked.

"The thing is, Emma, even in relationships without magic, you don't tell the person you're with everything, do you?"

"Actually, I do!" she said, lifting herself off of his chest.

"You don't have a small secret in the back of your mind?"

"Well..." she hesitated.

"That's what it's like. You have a relationship and you try not to go around telling your deep, dark secret."

"Oh."

"Emma, what we have right now, I want this to be something. I said it before, I think we can be something amazing."

Her heart stopped, she couldn't picture the time that he actually said that. Emma only knew that he'd told her in the dream she had that they could be something amazing. "Micah, the only time you said that to me was in a dream…"

"You were dreaming about me?" he joked.

"I'm serious. You said that exact same thing to me in a dream I had!"

"Emma, I'm sure that I've told you—we have the potential to be great together. You heard Ying, you're incredibly strong."

Emma sighed, but to say the exact words… "Yeah, about that…why were you two fighting?"

"It was nothing. Ying, she becomes very jealous…" Micah began.

"Were you two together?" Emma suddenly felt a little jealous. Micah reassuringly kissed her head and squeezed her tightly.

"I've been with her. Once. More than that, though, we worked together for a short time. She doesn't necessarily become jealous of other women, but of their powers. Ying tried to make herself stronger, but it only made her weaker. She can sense powers and that's it."

"So, is she 'dark'?"

"She is."

"Can you tell me about this darkness?"

"Well, what would you like to know?" he asked, smiling.

"Everything. I mean, what does it mean to be dark? Isn't it evil?" Emma was curious to know everything about being dark, especially if it was so important to Micah for her to turn.

"Emma, dark is anything but evil. I found since I went dark that I've become stronger."

"Really?" she asked, becoming more intrigued with this darkness.

"Yes. That's why I think that you should let the darkness in. Your powers will only get stronger." He grabbed her hand and kissed her knuckles.

"Does it take something special to be dark?"

"You need to let the darkness take over. There is something that is holding you back."

"I've tried to let it in," she argued.

"I know you're trying, but something is holding you back."

She shrugged, not knowing what else she could do to let this darkness in. Emma wanted nothing more than to be with Micah, and she hoped that nothing was holding her back. Lying back down on his chest, she tried to think of something more she could do to let him get closer. Emma closed her eyes as she listened to Micah's breathing, she felt relaxed with him.

***

"Emma, wake up. Your phone has been ringing off the hook," Micah whispered.

"Hmm? What time is it?" she grumbled, snuggling into the pillow. She'd never been so comfortable before.

"Quarter after nine," he answered, checking his clock on his nightstand.

Emma jolted up from the pillow. The full moon was glowing through his window, lighting the entire room. She hadn't even remembered falling asleep! She grabbed his sheet from the bed and ran toward her bag, pulling her phone from the bottom. Twelve missed calls, all from Kyle. Four texts, all from

Kyle, each one getting angrier.

Kyle: Where the hell are you? I thought we were doing dinner! Sushi is in the fridge. I'm going out.

Oh shit. Her heart dropped. She'd never stood up Kyle before. They had always managed to check in with each other. She hadn't talked to him all day and now she messed things up and pretty much stood him up for dinner. Emma dialed his number, hoping he would actually answer it and not be too mad at her.

"Where the hell are you?" Kyle seethed.

"Calm down. I'm fine, I'm over at Micah's. I fell asleep."

"Well, I got tired of waiting, so I'm having a beer at Matchboxes."

"Kyle, I'm so sorry. I really didn't mean to. Let me come buy you a drink." Emma felt horrible listening to him yell at her.

"No, I'm still pissed. I'll meet you at home." He then hung up on her. She'd seen Kyle mad once or twice before, but never at her. She didn't like being on the receiving end of his anger.

"You okay?" Micah asked, slipping on his pants.

"I don't know. I probably should catch a cab home."

"A cab? Emma, I'll take you home."

"Thank you," Emma whispered. She almost didn't want to go home and face Kyle.

She quickly dressed and Micah walked her to the passenger side of the SUV. He kissed her hand as he helped her in, then pushed the heater button on the seat. Emma smiled at the sweet gesture. As much as she enjoyed her time with Micah tonight, she was worried for the wrath of Kyle that waited for her at home.

Micah pulled up to the building and Emma sat there staring at the entrance, hesitant to get out.

"Do you want me to walk you up?" Micah asked.

"No, I think right now Kyle needs to have his time to yell at me," she said, shaking her head. As much as she wanted Micah to come up with her, she knew that it would only make it worse to have him around.

"You know you don't have to take that," Micah said sternly.

"I kind of deserve it. I was supposed to have dinner with him tonight." She sighed. She felt like she did deserve it. She had stood her friend up.

"I'm sure he'll get over it. Call me later." Micah leaned over the console and kissed her cheek.

"I will. Thank you for today, I had fun." She blushed.

"As did I. Are you at work tomorrow?"

"Unfortunately," she sulked. "I only have a few more days until I leave though."

"Leave?" he questioned.

"Yeah, I'm flying home for Christmas." Emma beamed.

"Oh, I see."

"Is everything all right?" she asked, grabbing his hand.

"Yes, I didn't think...I don't know. I have to work the club tomorrow night, so I'll come by and get some coffee beforehand."

"Okay." Emma smiled before she leaned in and gave him a kiss goodbye.

She walked slowly up the walkway, careful not to slip, and turned to wave to Micah as he drove off. She unlocked the door to see the lights were on and she could hear rummaging in the kitchen. Her heart felt like it was going ninety miles per hour, she was nervous with anticipation.

"Ky?" she called out.

"Yeah," he snapped, putting dishes away in the kitchen.

"I'm really sorry," she apologized quietly.

"So you said," he retorted. Kyle was never cold to her. She was not used to him snapping at her like this. She felt like there was a pit in her stomach.

"Can you stop for a second so we can talk?" she begged, grabbing his arm.

"What do you want me to say, Em?" He pulled his arm away and backed away from her.

"I don't know, but at least listen?" Emma pleaded. Tears began to sting her eyelids.

"Do you realize all the times I've been there for you?" Kyle shouted, causing Emma to startle.

"Of course, I know!" she began to sob.

"In all the years we've known each other, I've never *once* stood you up for a piece of ass."

"Kyle..." she started.

"No, not once. I made sure that I knew where my loyalties stood. You're my best friend, Emma, and I made sure the women I slept with knew that if you needed me that you came first. I wanted to do a dinner for just us two and you fucking ditched me."

110

"I...I don't know what happened! I fell asleep and I woke up and realized that I pretty much slept for nine hours!"

"Maybe your boyfriend drugged you too!" He slammed the cabinet door shut and walked out of the kitchen.

"That's not cool, Ky!"

"You're right, it's not cool! I'm going to bed."

"Wait! I'm not done!" Emma shouted.

"I am."

"Kyle, stop!" Emma shouted, and Kyle suddenly stopped. The room began to go black around her.

"Turn around!" His body quickly spun around.

"Emma, what the fuck are you doing?" he panicked.

"Trying to talk to you! You don't have any right to talk to me like that!" She lifted her hands to her chest, her palms facing Kyle and made a pushing motion, Kyle fell backwards.

"Fuck!" he screamed out, grabbing his wrist. "I think I just sprained my wrist!"

Suddenly the room got lighter and Emma snapped out of whatever trance she was in. "Oh my God!" She ran over to Kyle, who was lying on the floor. For that brief moment, she didn't feel anything like herself. "Are you okay?"

"Emma, there is something seriously fucked up about you." Kyle rubbed his wrist, moving it around to make sure it wasn't broken.

"I don't know what happened. I just saw black!"

"I think you need help," Kyle whispered as he pushed himself off the floor. He walked to his bedroom and slammed the door. What the hell just happened?

Chapter Ten

Locking herself in her room, Emma paced while trying to figure out what just happened as the tears began to stream down her face. Kyle was her best friend and she had just hurt him. Her heart was breaking in two and she felt like the air was knocked out of her. She finally sat down on the edge of the bed, letting the tears flow, when she heard a buzzing sound coming from her coat pocket.

"Hello?" she sobbed.

"Honey, are you okay?"

"Yeah, Mom. I...I just had a little fight with Kyle," Emma lied. She was miserable. "How are you?"

"Are you sure it was just a little fight?"

"Yep," Emma snapped.

"Well if you need to talk..." she began.

"No, I'm fine." All Emma really wanted to do was get off the phone with her mom and figure out how to make things right between her and Kyle.

"Oh. Well, I just was calling to say hi. I can tell

this isn't a good time, so I'll let you go," she said solemnly.

"Thanks, Mom. I'm sorry for snapping, I'll talk to you later. Love you."

"Love you too."

Emma hung up the phone and tried to come up with ways to apologize to Kyle. She quietly tapped on his door, but he didn't answer. She knew now was definitely not the time to try to talk to him. Tiptoeing back to her room, she turned off the light and crawled into bed. Her phone was on the nightstand and she noticed the notification light was blinking. She grabbed her phone off the table and opened the message.

Micah: I had an amazing time with you today. Call me tomorrow. Xox

The message from Micah made her a little happier. She plugged the phone into its charger and rolled over. This day had been absolutely crazy, so a good night's sleep was something she needed. Emma decided she would give Kyle the night to cool off.

***

"You're a good girl, doing what you're told," Micah said, kissing Emma's shoulder. The room was cold and dark. She was shivering as he wrapped his arms around her.

"I don't know how much more I can do!" she cried. Emma couldn't see much around her, but she

114

could see a woman lying on the ground.

"Once she's gone, Emma, you'll be a lot stronger than anyone. Your father will be so happy." His voice was so tense. She wanted to pull away from him, but he had a grip around her waist.

"My father?" she asked, trying to face him.

"Emma, don't you know anything about your past?"

"No, I guess I don't..." she started.

"Finish her off and I can tell you everything," another man spoke up from the corner. She tried to look at his face, but she couldn't make it out.

"Who is she?" Emma asked.

"Your mother," he stated. She felt the coldness of his hand as it touched her arm. Micah began to loosen his grip and back away. Emma didn't want him to leave.

"No!" she screamed.

"No!" Emma screamed again, jolting up in bed. "Oh my God, what the fuck?" She reached for her phone, dialing her mom's number. She had to make sure that her mom was okay, because that dream was too real. She felt a sharp pain in her side, the same one as the other night, but it quickly disappeared once her mom answered the phone.

"Hi. Are you and Kyle doing better?" she greeted.

"You're okay!" Emma shouted.

"Of course I'm okay. Why?" her mom answered, confused.

"I had the worst dream. You haven't talked to my...my dad, have you?" Emma rambled in a panic.

"Emma? Are you okay?" she asked worriedly.

"I'm fine," she sighed, rubbing her hand over her face. She hadn't asked about her dad. Ever. Emma couldn't believe that she just asked that question out of the blue.

"To answer your question, no. Why do you ask?" her mom asked defensively.

"It was just in my dream. It was just very realistic and it scared me, that's all," Emma explained.

"Emma…" she started. Emma could tell that she was worried.

"Yeah?" Was there something that her mom was hiding?

"Nothing. Are you okay?"

"Things have just been a little weird, but I'm sure I'm okay."

"Well, I need to go open the store. Call me later. Have a good day."

"Thanks, Mom. Bye." Hanging up the phone, she wiped the few beads of sweat off of her forehead. That was the most intense dream she'd ever had, and the fact that her mom was in it really began to scare her. She really wanted to call in sick to work, but she didn't think that it would go over well. Emma pushed herself out of bed and booted up her laptop. She needed to apologize to Kyle, but she didn't know where to even begin. She pulled up her emails and just typed out a simple message.

Kyle,
I'm really sorry about last night.
Can we talk?

He quickly responded.

Emma,
Now is not a good time. I'm at work.

Her heart began to race. She needed to talk to him, so she continued with the next email.

Kyle,
I'm really sorry! I never meant to hurt you. I just saw black and I don't know what happened.

She pressed *send*. Hoping for a response, she began to chew on her thumb nail.

Emma,
You didn't even touch me. I'm not one to get scared, but, Em, this shit fucking scared the hell outta me. I don't know what I'm really supposed to say.

She began to cry again. She couldn't lose her best friend. Kyle was her *only* friend. As she grabbed a tissue, another email appeared.

Em,
I'm flying out today after work. I thought about it last night and I think until this shit gets figured out, I'm going to give you some space.

Her heart stopped. Emma didn't even know what

to say. She nervously typed.

Kyle,
Are you coming back?

When he didn't respond right away, she thought she was going to have a complete nervous breakdown.

Em,
Of course I'm coming back. You're my friend, I just think that you need to figure out what is going on with you and get it fixed. Stop crying.

She chuckled at the 'stop crying' part of his message. He really did know her all too well.

I'm not crying! I love ya and I'm really sorry.

She pressed *send,* feeling a little better about the situation, even if he was leaving early to give her 'space.' She really did need to figure out how to control these powers. It was not going to be good for anyone if she got so upset that she could hurt someone. Just as Emma was going to shut her laptop down, another email chimed in.

P.S.
Coffee is made in the pot. Try not to have too much fun without me. I'll be home after New Year's. Love ya too.

She was now crying happy tears. Emma shut her

laptop down and went to make herself a cup of coffee. As she poured the hot cup of joe into her mug, she heard her phone ringing back in the room. She grabbed her cup and quickly walked back to see Micah's name on the caller ID.

"Hello?" she answered, smiling.

"Good morning. Do you have work today?" Micah asked.

"I do," she sulked. "Are you going to be at the club?"

"Just for a bit, so maybe I can take you to lunch?"

"That'd be nice," she said warily.

"Everything all right?"

"Yeah, just a fight between me and Kyle," Emma sighed. She wasn't sure she wanted to tell Micah about what happened.

"Sorry to hear that. Was it about last night?"

"Yeah, but I think we've got it on the mend. It's just hard, he's my best friend."

"Well, I'm here if you need to talk," Micah offered.

"Thanks, Micah, I appreciate that. Anyway, I usually go to lunch around twelve thirty."

"I'll be there."

"See ya later." Emma was grinning from ear to ear. She really did find a great guy and it made it even better that he understood her.

"Goodbye, Emma."

They hung up and she suddenly felt like a new person. His voice was incredibly soothing and the fact he was willing to help made her feel a bit better. Turning on her TV, she had a little over an hour until her shift started, she flipped through some channels while sipping on her coffee.

After she finished off her coffee, Emma quickly dressed and grabbed her coat and bag. Today was going to be a good day after all.

The coffee shop was dead when she arrived. Casey was on shift and cleaning out one of the cupboards. She waved to him as she headed back to the office to clock in and set down her things.

"Hey, Emma," Casey greeted.

"Hey, how are things?" Emma said cheerily. It was rare that Casey would greet her so she was hoping he was going to be in a good mood all day.

"Been slow. Are you working the twenty-third?" he asked, placing some cups on the counter.

"No, I'll be out of town. I'm flying home to see my mom. Why?" She could see his face drop into a frown.

"Oh, I was gonna see if you could work my shift. I have a party to go to. Oh well, I'll be fashionably late."

"Sorry," Emma apologized. She was expecting more of an argument, but when it didn't happen she was sort of relieved.

"No worries. Well, now that you're here, I was instructed to clean out all of our cabinets and make sure that all of our Christmas swag is out on the floor from the backroom."

"All right, I'll start there."

Wandering toward the back, she gathered up what she could carry of the Christmas décor and merchandise. As Emma walked back up to the front of the store she could hear Casey speaking to someone in the lobby. "I don't even know why they keep her here. She never works."

"Can't they just fire her?" an unknown male huffed.

"I wish they would. She can be *such* a bitch."

"Well, maybe that can be your Christmas bonus, ask to cut loose ends. Hey, babe, I need to go. I'll see you later tonight."

Emma almost dropped everything in her hands. She'd worked at this shop for a little longer than him, and now she was the loose end? Her heart began to pound against her chest. She had worked more overtime, cleaned more than her share of the shop. She'd never been friends with Casey, but she sure as hell respected him. She was actually feeling more hurt than she was pissed. Taking a few deep breaths, Emma finally rounded the corner.

"Oh, you found it," Casey said, smirking.

"Yep. Where it's always been." She inhaled and tried to calm myself. "Hey, Casey, what's your problem?"

"Excuse me?" he scoffed.

"Well, I could hear you talking shit about me." Emma clenched her jaw as she watched him.

He rolled his eyes. "Emma, what I said wasn't for you to hear, but since you did—I meant it."

"How do you figure?" She began to get angry. He was fine with the fact he was talking shit about her and didn't care she heard. Not even offering an apology?

"You're always taking time off. I find that I'm covering a lot of shifts and you don't even step up. I'm just seeing the way you are, and quite frankly, I find you lazy."

Emma tried to take a few breaths before she said anything she'd regret, but she couldn't help the rage that was beginning to build inside of her.

"You're nothing but a selfish prick. You don't care about anyone but yourself and that needs to change," Emma said, gritting her teeth. She threw everything she'd been holding down on the floor—mugs, holiday coffee flavors, and decorations. Her hands felt that surge of energy and one by one she levitated the items up in the air, over her head. Emma began to see nothing but black, like last night with Kyle.

"Jesus, what the hell are you doing?" he screamed.

"You scared?" Emma chuckled, but it didn't sound like her laugh. She felt like she was watching someone else. It was like an out-of-body experience.

"Yes!" he yelled. "Oh God, stop!"

"Good." She smiled, lifting more of the coffees up from their displays and began to fling them at Casey. "Fuck you and this job. I quit." Emma raised her hand and her coat and bag came flying out from the back. She swished her hand, so she could open the door, and walked out.

As Emma walked down the street, she began to feel different and became more aware of what she had just done. She just quit her only job. Emma quickly dialed up Micah—she had no idea what to do.

"Hello?" Micah answered.

"Hey, so, I…lunch…" Emma stuttered.

"Emma, what's wrong?"

"Something's happened and I'm on my way home."

"Shit, I'll be right there," he said, hanging up the phone. Emma walked a little bit faster toward her apartment.

As she walked up the stairs, Micah's Lexus pulled up alongside the curb. "Are you hurt?" he asked, running up to her.

"No, I...I just quit my job. I have no idea what the fuck I'm going to do, To be honest with you, I don't know why I did it."

"You don't know why you quit your job?" he asked, running his fingers through her hair.

"Exactly. I...I kinda blacked out and quit."

"You blacked out?"

"Well, it's hard to explain...it happened last night with Kyle too. I don't 'black out' per se, 'cause I can still see and am there, but am I going insane?"

"No, you're not going insane. Let's get you out of the cold."

"Micah, you said you're like me! *Help* me!"

"Emma, you heard it yourself. You're very strong and your powers can do a lot of things. You just have to try to gain control. I can't say that I've ever had this problem, as I'm not as strong as you. I don't know what to say." He pulled her into him, leading her up the stairs. It really was too cold to stand outside *and* try to figure out what was going on.

Chapter Eleven

After they removed their shoes and coats, they settled onto the couch. There were so many questions going through Emma's head. Mainly, she wondered what the hell was really going on as Micah pulled her in close, covering them with a blanket that was laid across the top of the couch. His breathing was calm and it sounded soothing as she rested her head on his chest. Suddenly there was a rap at the front door. She hadn't been expecting anyone, so her heart began to race.

"Who is it?" Emma asked, walking to the door.

"Denver PD," the male voice answered.

The cops! Why would they even be at her place? Emma quickly opened the door. "Good afternoon, Officer. What can I help you with?"

"Are you Emma Blackwood?" the officer asked sternly. His face looked emotionless.

"Yes, sir," she answered nervously.

"Do you work at the coffee shop around the corner?"

"Y-yes," Emma stuttered. Was she being

arrested?

"Were you working about thirty minutes ago?"

Micah quickly appeared next to her, interrupting, "Officer, can you tell us what is going on?"

"I'm sorry, you are?" the officer asked.

"Micah Oliver. I've been with Ms. Blackwood for this whole morning."

"Well, Mr. Oliver, we have a complaint from a Casey Perkins that she was at the shop and assaulted him, damaging merchandise in the process."

"I…" Emma began.

"Officer, Mr. Perkins has been out to get my girlfriend for some time now. However, I can reassure you she was with me this entire time. Were there any witnesses?"

The officer reviewed his notes and shook his head. She knew they wouldn't have any proof on tape, because the security cameras had been out for the last month, so that gave her a little relief. Emma, however, was a little shocked, because not only did Micah refer to her as his girlfriend, but he was also lying to the police for her. Emma stood there, listening to the two begin to talk as if she wasn't there. The officer agreed to look into it further and reached out to shake Micah's hand. Micah then gripped the officer's hand tighter and the look on the officer's face began to change. He went from stern to happy, as if Micah had used some sort of powers on the officer during the handshake.

"Good afternoon, both of you. Sorry to have bothered you," the officer said, walking out the front door.

Emma locked the door behind him and walked back to Micah. "What the hell was that?" she asked.

"It was obviously about what happened earlier. Casey was scared and called the police," Micah stated.

"I got that much. What I'm asking is, how was the officer not buying a word of your story, then suddenly he was bidding us a good afternoon?" Emma was sure she was going to be arrested.

"I told you before, Emma, I have powers too. I simply persuaded him to believe that you've been here with me. Unless you'd rather me call him back and you go to jail for assault and vandalism."

"No, no. Thank you, I really appreciate you saving my ass."

"Well, it's a great ass to save."

Walking to him, she smiled widely. "We have the whole place to ourselves," Emma hinted.

"I'd like to see what happens when you let your powers out."

"I don't know if I want to…"

"You won't hurt me, Emma."

"What if I do?" she asked nervously. She really didn't want anything to hurt him, and with these little blackout spells, she didn't know what she was capable of.

"I can take care of myself. Let's see." Micah grabbed her hands, squeezing them. "I promise, you won't hurt me." He kissed each hand, looking deeply into her eyes before kissing her softly on the lips. "I trust you, Emma."

"All right…" She took a few steps away from him, hoping that she wouldn't hurt him. Emma closed her eyes and began to think of the things she heard Casey say about her. Unfortunately, the feeling she was having in the coffee shop had receded and nothing was happening.

"What's the matter?" he asked.

"Nothing's happening," she sighed. She didn't know what she had to do to get her powers to start working.

"Most times, Emma, our powers are based off our emotions. Clear your head and concentrate on something that will really build up your emotions. I want you to close your eyes. Take a deep breath. Now, clear your head of everything," he instructed.

Emma tried to clear her head of everything that was distracting her. The only thought that wouldn't leave her mind was her mom lying helpless on the floor. The tears in her eyes began to prick and she felt the feeling, once again, in the palms of her hands. Clamping her eyes shut, Emma lifted her arms in the air. The vision was becoming stronger and she could see that male figure in the back of the room. She tried to move things out of the way to see him more clearly.

"Emma! Stop!" Micah yelled.

Her eyes opened and she fell back onto the couch. "What happened?" she asked, rubbing her temples.

"You had everything in this room suspended in the air, including me. I could honestly say that I felt the air leaving my body…" He swallowed, sitting down next her.

"Micah! I'm so sorry! I knew that this was a bad idea," Emma said, wiping the tears from her eyes.

"Emma, don't apologize, you're very strong and I can help you with your powers. Do you know how you got them to work?"

"I started to concentrate on something that upset me. A dream that I had last night." She placed her head in her hands. "So, how are you going to help me? I mean, how do I control this if I get upset? I can't go around hurting people!" Emma looked up at Micah, searching his face for answers.

"With a lot of help…we'll get you to understand it a lot better." Micah grabbed his throat and began to rub. "He's gonna have a harder time than I thought," he mumbled, looking at the floor as he rubbed his head.

"What? Who?"

"Nothing, sorry, just mumbling to myself. I'm gonna grab some water, can I get you something?"

"No, I'm fine." She shook her head, leaning back onto the couch. The last time she'd seen her dad she was really young. She remembered bits and pieces of him, but didn't remember exactly what he looked like. The man standing in the back of the room looked like the blur—maybe a bit older—of her dad. She was starting to become a little concerned.

Micah came back to the living room with two glasses of water. "I know you said that you didn't want anything, but I think that you should drink some water."

After having two episodes, she did feel a little dehydrated. Taking a large gulp, she placed the glass on the end table and turned to Micah, who was watching her intently. "Micah, take my mind off what happened," she insisted, straddling him. Their lips met as his hands grabbed her hair, pulling her toward him. Her hands desperately pawed at his clothes, trying to unbutton each button.

His hands pulled her t-shirt up over her head, interrupting her from getting his last button undone. After unhooking her bra, he quickly tossed it across the room. His lips gently kissed both of her nipples. Emma's head fell back, enjoying the feel of his tongue tracing up her chest. He slowly lowered her to the floor, pulling off her jeans. Standing up, Micah snapped his fingers and the fireplace ignited. She smiled up at him as he pulled down his pants before kneeling over her. "How is it that we have only known each other for a few days, but I feel like we've known each other forever?" Emma asked as he slowly entered her.

"Maybe we have," he breathed, smiling.

"You think?"

"Maybe in a previous life we did." He pushed hard into her while kissing her neck. Each time she had been with Micah, it seemed like they were just going to be friends with benefits. Suddenly every move, every kiss…felt different. "Emma…" He paused, kissing her, but didn't continue. Micah pushed harder into her and she dug her nails into his back, moaning out. Were things suddenly different now that it was more than just sex?

As they both slowly began to climax, the fire's flames grew brighter and bigger. Even with the softest of touches, he seemed so intense. She didn't want it to end.

***

"You okay?" Micah asked before taking a sip of his water. He placed the cup back onto the coffee table, returning to Emma as they cuddled underneath a blanket in front of the fireplace.

"Yeah," she nodded, snuggling into his chest.

"You're awfully quiet." His fingers traced up and down her back.

"Just...trying to take everything in, I guess."

"Once you learn that you are anything but 'normal' anymore, it's a whole new experience," he reassured her, placing a small kiss on the top of her head.

"You're telling me! Have you known your whole life?" Emma asked, lifting her head to look at him.

"I found out in middle school. I was picked on in seventh grade, and I imagined the kid getting hit in the face with a chair and before I knew it, a chair was flying across the room, smacking him in the face."

"Oh my God!" Emma's jaw dropped. She couldn't imagine being a child and having such power.

"Yeah, I went home and told my dad."

"What'd he do?" she asked anxiously.

"He beat the shit out of me." He sighed, running his fingers through her hair.

She looked at him in disbelief. "What?"

"Yeah, he was a drunk. My mom apparently was a witch and my dad wasn't anything. Literally. She told me that I had powers. I just wasn't going to be as strong because my dad wasn't of any sort of power." He seemed uncomfortable talking about his past.

"So…you think that my parents have these types of powers?"

"It's possible. It could be some sort of ancestor who has powers."

"Huh. My mom…" Emma stopped, trying to recall any sort of memory of her mom talking to her about this sort of thing. "Well, my mom never mentioned anything, but I don't know my dad. He left when I was little, but I really don't remember anything about him."

"That's a shame. You're becoming really powerful," he said, smiling. "And most parents don't, unless they're put on the spot."

"So, when you said 'in a previous life,' do you believe in that?" she asked, propping herself up on her elbow.

"Yeah, I think it's possible. I don't know for sure, though." They lay there staring deep into each other's eyes. Emma never believed in past lives, but the connection between them was enough for her to start.

"What time is it?" Emma asked, yawning.

"I'm not sure. I should probably head out though. I left work before getting anything done."

"I'm sorry." She felt bad that she had pulled him away from his work.

"For? I had to make sure you were okay," he said, smiling.

"Thank you again," Emma whispered before leaning over and kissing him.

Micah slowly rolled over, grabbing his pants and slipping them on as he stood up. Emma watched as he dressed, contemplating if she should do the same

131

as she was rather warm just huddled under the blanket. He knelt down and softly kissed her lips. "I need to go to the club tonight, but if you need me call me right away."

"I think I'll be fine." With all these new powers, Emma felt like she could protect herself.

"Good night, Emma. I'll see you later?"

"Bye, Micah. I'd love that."

"Don't forget to lock your door after I leave."

"I think I can manage that." She winked, watching him head for the door and slip on his coat. As the door shut behind him, she snapped her fingers, hearing the door lock. She lay back on the floor, smiling.

Chapter Twelve

"This is so frustrating!" Emma huffed. It felt like with each hour they spent working together, the stronger she was getting, which meant she needed more help to learn how to control her powers. Being around *him* made her feel more powerful.

"Don't worry, it will get better. I promise," Micah said, sweeping up the last pieces of a mug. They had been working on bringing objects toward her and the mugs seemed like a good idea, until she started breaking them.

"I hope so, 'cause I've just about destroyed all of my coffee mugs! Kyle is going to be pissed when he comes home and sees that there are no more mugs for coffee." She chuckled as she sat down on the couch. "How did you learn to control yours? Or did it just come naturally?"

"I had to work on it just as hard as you. I'd get angry and use my powers to slam doors and they'd crack the frame. Granted, my mom was sympathetic, but when you have an alcoholic dad— he's not so kind. After a lot of hard work and concentration, I was able to control it and use them at the right time." Micah sat down on the couch next to her, pulling her into him.

"So, what am I doing wrong?"

"Emma, you're not doing anything wrong. You've only just started to learn about your powers and it's going to take time."

"Yeah, but with my trip out to see my mom coming up...I really don't want to have some sort of moment."

"Don't worry, when you start to feel it coming on, you can try to concentrate on something... soothing to you."

"What do I need to work on, then?" She really wanted to have everything under control before she had to fly across the country. She didn't want to worry about any sort of outburst of powers that could get her in trouble.

"First, the best thing to do is breathe. The moment your powers start to build up, you hold your breath. Take a few deep breaths before anything happens."

"Breathing. Check."

"The next part can't just be learned right away. Breathing is obviously a quick fix, but this part took me years to work on..."

"What is it?" she asked anxiously.

"You have to become in tune with all of your senses."

"I'm not sure I understand. I know I can see, hear, taste, feel, and smell." Emma was slightly confused. She was sure that she was in tune with all of her senses already.

"It's not just that. You have to understand each one. When someone is blind, they become more in tune with their other senses. Their hearing, touch—all of them are more sensitive. Since you have all of your senses available and working, you need to know how to connect with each one. I'm not that great of a teacher, 'cause I can't really explain it."

"Micah, you've been a great teacher. I really appreciate your help," she said, cupping his face and placing a soft kiss on his lips. "Oh, so I hate to ask you…"

"What's that?"

"I need to go into work and collect my paycheck. Could you possibly come with me?"

"Of course! Grab your coat, let's go," Micah said, grabbing his coat.

Even though Micah had a really warm car, they decided to walk to the coffee shop. She enjoyed being cuddled up to him. Her nerves were getting the best of her, though, as they neared the entrance. She hadn't talked to or seen Casey since she quit. As they walked in, Casey started to look a little panicked behind the counter.

"Emma. Umm…w-what are y-you doing here?" he stuttered.

"I just need to pick up my paycheck."

"Oh. I-I think it's in the back. I'll go get it."

"Thanks." She turned to Micah. "I should've just had them mail it to me. I'm worried he's gonna call the cops again."

"I'll handle it," Micah reassured her, rubbing her back. Casey came around the corner with a white envelope in his hands. He tossed it across the

135

counter. "Are you Casey?" Micah asked, stepping toward the counter. Emma's heart was racing.

"Yeah? Who are you?"

"Micah Oliver," he said, holding out his right hand. Casey reached over to shake it. "I'm the owner of Ominous and I would love to have you as a guest." Micah's grip on Casey's hand became tighter. Casey began to struggle to get out of the handshake, but started to slowly become more at ease. Micah pulled him over the counter, enough to lean in and whisper something into his ear. Casey pulled back and nodded.

"Emma! I'm sorry that you had to leave us," Casey said. His tone of voice had changed drastically.

"Uh...I'm sorry too," she lied. Emma wasn't sure exactly what had happened.

"Well, come and visit me soon." Casey smiled as he waved at her and Micah.

"Okay..." Emma said. Micah picked up the envelope and handed it to her as they walked out the front door. "Do I even dare ask?"

"Just a little magic," Micah replied, winking. Emma wanted this man more than ever now. She *had* to get him back to her apartment.

It wasn't long before they arrived back to her place. As soon as they walked through the front door, Micah didn't hesitate to quickly remove all of her clothes. She was barely able to shut the door before he carried her to the bedroom. "I want you so bad!" Emma whispered into his ear.

"Emma, I can't wait to be inside you," he breathed.

***

Lying in her bed, Emma felt so right with Micah. Sure, things seemed rushed between them, but at the same time, they clicked. His breathing was calm and he had fallen asleep. Her head was lying on the pillow next to him, while her fingers combed through his thick, black hair.

As she traced her fingers down the side of his face, he startled awake. "I'm sorry, I didn't mean to wake you," she whispered.

"I didn't mean to fall asleep." He lifted his head, looking over her shoulder to check the time.

"Do you have to go? I'd really like you to stay." Emma felt like she was looking a little desperate, but Micah pulled her closer to him. "Can I ask you something?"

"Sure," he said, trying to hide a yawn.

"Do you...I don't know, think that we're moving too fast?"

His body tensed slightly. "Moving fast? How so?"

"Micah, we've known each other for a couple weeks. We've spent a lot of time together and...I don't know, I feel like we are..."

"Getting serious?"

"Yes. And I don't want to rush things, so..."

"Emma, things have definitely moved really fast. I'm not going to lie, I usually don't date. I have so much going on in my life with the multiple clubs, which is enough to keep things to a bare minimum."

"Oh..." Emma started.

"But with you...you're just someone who I want

to spend time with. When we're together, I don't care about what's going on with my clubs. I realized I have managers who are there to handle things. I've never been around anyone like you, Emma. When I see something I like, I go after it. I want you, and if it feels like we're rushing things, it's because I want all of you. I don't care how fast it feels."

Her heart stopped. Never in her life had any guy made her heart skip a beat more than he had. She now, more than ever, felt like he was the one she was supposed to be with. Emma rolled on top of him and straddled him. She needed to feel him inside her again.

***

Sex was no longer *just* sex. It seemed as if having powers brought out a more adventurous side of Emma in the bedroom. Before Micah, she rarely had sex outside of the bedroom. Emma would've been considered boring, but now she'd covered every square inch—except Kyle's room—of her apartment. Her favorite, by far, was being pushed up against the wall. He would lift her with his powers, making things more erotic.

As the end of the week approached, she became more aware that Kyle wasn't home. It had been awfully quiet the last few days, and without him there to order pizza and drink beers with, it made her incredibly depressed. She sat on the couch, flipping through the television channels as she contemplated calling him. She sent him a text instead.

Emma: It's Friday night...I miss pizza night with my best friend...

Not a minute later, her phone began to ring.

"Hey, I miss pizza night with my best friend too," Kyle said as Emma answered.

"I'm still really sorry, Kyle."

"Em...it'll be okay. I was scared outta my mind, but I can't imagine what's going through yours."

"I'm working on controlling it, but I had a little problem..."

"Problem?" Kyle interrupted. Emma had forgotten he had no idea about what happened, and her stomach dropped.

"Yeah, I'll tell you about it when you get back. You're still coming back after New Year's?"

"Yeah. Did you ask your mom about what's been going on?"

"No. I'm gonna when I get out there."

"Emma, she can probably help. Being the owner of a bookstore, maybe she knows something?"

"Possibly." After talking to Micah about his powers and how his parents knew about them, she didn't want to tell Kyle that her mom probably knew more than just something she read in a book. "How's home?" Emma asked, changing the subject.

"It hasn't changed, but this time my mom isn't being an evil hag. I think since my dad died, she's trying to be a bit nicer. It's kinda annoying," he chuckled.

"Well, try to have fun. I'm thinking that I'm going to order my own pizza and eat it all."

"You'll get a bigger ass."

"What? My ass isn't big!" Emma shouted, trying to get a glimpse of her ass.

"Have you seen it lately?" Kyle laughed.

"Dick!" she chuckled.

"Miss ya, Emma."

"Miss you too. I'll talk to you later."

"Bye."

She hung up the phone, feeling somewhat better. As she started to dial the pizza place, her phone began to ring again. Had Kyle forgotten something? The number came up as blocked.

"Hello?" There was no sound on the other line. Her heart began to race. "Hello?" she asked again.

"Dearest Emma…"

"Who is this?" Her palms began to sweat as she gripped the phone tighter.

"I hear that you're really coming along."

"Look, mister, I don't know who you are, bu…" she started.

"Maybe you don't know me, but I know you," he said emotionlessly.

"How'd you get my number?" Emma asked. Her heart began to beat faster and she was officially freaked out.

"Stop talking and just listen!" he shouted as she was ready to hang up. Emma let out a small sigh. "Good girl. Now, as I was saying, you're really coming along. Your powers are getting stronger and I think you'll be a great asset to me. I'll be contacting you again. Soon."

"*Who are you?*" Emma screamed into the handset. The line went dead. She tossed her phone across the couch, staring at it as if it was some sort of demon. His voice was so cold, and yet, had some familiar tone to it. She stood up and began to pace around the apartment, turning all the lights on as she passed each room, checking to make sure that she was the only one in the apartment.

A knock at the door suddenly made her stomach fly into her mouth. "Who is it?" she hollered, grabbing a pair of scissors from the junk drawer in the kitchen.

"Emma, its Micah," the voice said. She sighed in relief. Running to the door, she quickly opened it. As he walked in, she threw herself into his arms. "Are you okay?"

"Just had a really strange phone call, it kinda scared me. Okay, that was a lie—it didn't kinda scare me, I'm really freaked out!" she said shakily.

"Who was it?" he panicked.

"Some guy. I think he's been watching me and knows about my powers!"

"Did he say who he was?" he repeated.

"No, but I'm really freaked out. I've been really careful not to use my powers in public and when I'm practicing my blinds are shut. Micah, this is really fucking weird."

"Well, I'm here now," he consoled, kissing the top of her head. She could hear his heart racing. She didn't mean to worry him.

"I thought you had to work at the club tonight."

"I do. It's still early, so I thought I'd stop by first. I'm glad I did." Micah leaned in and gave her a soft kiss on her temple. "I want you to come with me tonight."

"I…"

"I don't want to worry about you all night, so go get dressed," he ordered, turning her around and pushing her toward her room. Emma browsed through all of her clothes, but had no idea what she was going to wear. In the end, she grabbed a black and white, spaghetti-strapped top along with a pair of jeans. "Emma, are you ready?"

"Seriously? I just started dressing!"

"You have powers," he joked.

"I…" She stopped. He was right. She'd never thought of using them to get ready. Where was this power when she was running late for all her classes in college? But in the end, she was only able to move a brush through her hair. She needed a lot more practice to do more than one thing at once.

Once she was finished, she walked into the living room where Micah was sitting on the couch waiting for her. A devilish smile appeared on his face as he stood up. "You look…sexy."

"Thank you. I'm ready when you are."

"Let's go have some fun." Micah helped her into her coat as they made their way out of the apartment.

***

The club was just as packed as it was on the night of the grand opening. The only difference was the lack of shouting reporters and photographers. Micah had to do a bit of work, so Emma told him he could find her either at the bar, or on the dance floor.

Ordering a beer, Emma sat down at the bar and

watched all the people dancing. As she looked around, she could see a waving hand from across the room. She couldn't tell if the person was waving at her, so she tried to ignore it. When the person came closer, she noticed that it was Damon waving at her.

"Hey, Emma. How are ya?" Damon asked, taking a seat next to her at the bar.

"Damon! I'm good, how are you?" Emma hadn't seen him since the opening of the club. She'd meant to call him or go down to Kyle's office to see him.

"Doing good. You know, livin' the dream," he chuckled, obviously having had a few drinks.

"About the other night...are you okay?"

"Yeah, I'm good. I guess I stumbled backwards and looked like an idiot in front of a lot of people."

Emma gave him a puzzled look, either he hadn't remembered it or he was just trying to play it off. "You didn't look like an idiot and I don't think anyone saw. Mind if I ask a question?"

"If you let me buy you a drink," he said, winking at her.

"I think I can let you do that." Emma smiled, turning back around on the stool.

Damon waved the bartender over. "I'll have Jack on the rocks and the lovely lady will have?"

"Another beer, please." The bartender nodded at Emma and she gave him a smile.

Damon scooted closer. "Okay, so what's your question?" he asked. His hand moved to the back of her seat. She felt a little nervous being so close to him.

"The night of the opening, I was talking to Kyle

143

and I saw you and Micah...you both looked like you were about to throw punches. What was that?"

"I'm not sure. I was asking some questions, and then I asked about you and I guess that set him off."

"About me?" Why would Damon want to ask questions about her?

"Yeah, I was hoping that maybe you were just working with him and not his date. I really wanted to get your number that night...maybe take you out."

"Damon..." Emma began.

"Nah, it's cool. I got to buy you a drink tonight." He smiled, taking a sip of his whiskey.

"Care to dance?"

Emma looked around to see if Micah was anywhere near. She knew that it would only cause drama, but she didn't want to turn the poor guy down. "Sure," she nervously replied, sliding off the seat.

Damon grabbed her hand and led her onto the dance floor. They began to dance along to the beat of the music, but as she spun around, pressing her back into Damon, she felt a hand grab her wrist.

"Having fun?" Micah asked coldly.

"Micah! I..." Emma's heart stopped. He looked so angry with her.

He then turned to face Damon. "Mr. Ryder, I hope that you're enjoying your evening as well."

"Thanks, I am. And it's Damon, please," Damon scoffed.

"Wonderful. Well, Damon, I'm going to take my girlfriend away now." Micah reached for Emma's arm but she pulled away from him.

"Micah! I'm sorry, but I was just dancing," Emma snapped.

"With a guy who wants nothing more than to fuck you and never call?" Micah shouted over the music.

"What?" Damon and Emma both bellowed.

"I need to grab some things out of my office and you're coming with me. Good night, Damon," Micah said, pulling Emma with him. Damon started to walk after them, but one of the bouncers had appeared out of the crowd, holding his arm back.

Emma waved to Damon as he gave her a look of disappointment. Micah and Emma made their way behind the bar to a back staircase, leading up to an office that overlooked the entire dance floor. Now she knew how he saw where she was.

"What's your problem? Why would you say something like that?" Emma snapped. She was beyond embarrassed by Micah's little fit.

"Emma, I can sometimes read peoples thoughts."

"I thought you said you couldn't read minds!"

"I can't, but if I shake their hand or touch them, I can sometimes see a brief glimpse of what they're thinking."

"So…" Emma couldn't wait to hear his excuse.

"So, when you introduced me to your friend out there…all I saw was your naked body."

"This is ridiculous! You were probably imagining what we'd just done before we left!"

"Emma, it was Damon with you, his hands all over your body. Touching you. Feeling you. It was him."

Emma took a seat on the edge of the desk,

having a hard time processing all of this. If she was asked to believe him a month ago, she would have stomped out of the room, said he was crazy, and considered a restraining order. But since she had learned a new side of herself, she felt so confused. "So...you touched my arm when we first met. What did you see then?"

"I saw someone who was hurt, emotionally," Micah confessed. Emma's eyes dropped to the floor, and he was right. That night, she just wanted to drink away any thought of men. "And when I kissed you after dinner, all I could see was you and me." Lifting her chin, Micah looked deep into her eyes and leaned in and kissed her. "I just want to keep you safe, Emma," he whispered. Emma wrapped her arms around his waist and at that moment, she felt incredibly safe.

***

The rest of the weekend, Micah and Emma spent most of their free time together. Her mom had called on Sunday night, making sure Emma had everything that she needed for her trip home. Her mom had heard Micah in the background and started with the twenty questions. Emma reassured her mom that she would fill her in as soon as she arrived.

After hanging up with her, Emma grabbed a couple of wine glasses and the bottle that Micah had brought over earlier in the day. She walked into the living room to find Micah on his phone, but he quickly ended the call when she entered the room.

"Everything okay?" Emma asked, setting the glasses down on the table.

"Yeah, just work. Some underage kids were trying to get in tonight." He sighed.

"Oh. Do you need to go?"

"No, it was handled."

"Do other people at the club have powers?" she asked, pouring wine into their glasses.

"What made you think that?"

"I was just wondering."

"My bartender, Felix, does, and one of my bouncers. Everyone else, I guess, is normal."

Taking a sip of the wine, she snuggled into the couch. "What can they do?"

"Well, Felix..." Micah was interrupted by a knock at the door.

"I wonder who the hell that could be," Emma said, looking at the time. Eleven forty-five. She quietly made her way to the front door, peeking through the eyehole. She only saw what appeared to be a bottle label. She unlocked the door, slightly opened it, and found Zoe leaning up against it, holding a bottle of rum. She almost fell inside as Emma opened the door. She was three sheets to the wind. "Zoe? What are you doing here?"

"I...I forgot something in Kyle's room," she slurred.

"How did you get here? You're obviously drunk!"

"Kyl...I mean, Jennie drove me. Can I go grab my..." Zoe burped and Emma thought she was going to puke on the front door. Zoe pushed her way through and ran into Kyle's room, shutting the door.

"What is she doing?" Emma asked Micah as she walked toward Kyle's room.

"I don't know. It doesn't sound good though." He shrugged, trying to listen in through the bedroom door.

A loud crash came from within the room and Emma quickly swung the door open. Zoe had trashed Kyle's once really tidy room. "Zoe! What the fuck?" Emma screamed, using her powers to grab Kyle's speaker from Zoe's hand. Emma quickly looked at Micah, slightly impressed with herself.

"How did you do that?" she asked as she dropped down onto the bed and started to cry. "Did you know he broke up with me today?"

"What?"

"He called me. Out of the blue he says things aren't going the way he wants them to. Who's he sleeping with?"

"Zoe, honestly, I had no idea. I haven't talked to him since Friday."

"Really?"

Emma didn't know what to say. Even if she knew Kyle was sleeping with someone else, she wouldn't rat him out. Kyle was like her brother, and even though she was an only child, she knew the sibling rules. "Zoe, I think that you should go home," Emma said quietly.

"Emma! We were like besties!"

"Are you for real? Zoe, you...look, I'm gonna get mean, so you need to leave." Emma began to feel her powers at the tips of her fingers. Micah must have sensed it, because he placed his hand on the lower part of her back. Emma slowly felt it ease away.

"Emma, will you try to talk to him, please? I really liked him," she pleaded.

"Yeah. I'll do that," Emma lied, showing her to the front door.

"Really? You'll talk to him?" she asked hopefully.

"Yeah, sure," she lied again, shutting the door. As Emma turned around, Micah was chuckling at her. "What?" She giggled.

"Nothing like getting her hopes up. I'm proud of you, though."

"For?" she asked, walking into the living room.

"You had a lot of control over yourself."

"You helped…" Emma said seductively. Micah walked over to her and wrapped a hand around her waist. His other hand combed through her hair, pulling it over to expose her neck as he placed soft kisses followed by a gentle bite.

"Now that you've been good, time to get bad," he whispered in her ear before picking her up and carrying her into the bedroom.

Chapter Thirteen

"She did what?" Kyle shouted through the receiver.

"Why didn't you tell me that you broke up with her?" Emma asked, looking around Kyle's room to make sure Zoe didn't do any sort of damage to anything.

"I'm gonna fuckin' kill her. How bad is it? Besides, we weren't really official…"

"She just threw stuff around. She was about to throw your speakers…wait, what do you mean not official?"

"Oh please, dear God, she didn't fuck up my babies?" Kyle begged.

"No, I got in there just before she tossed one. So, are you gonna tell me what happened?"

"Just being out here. I went out with a few guys that I knew from back in the day. The pussy was just all around and I didn't want to keep turnin' it down. I really thought about trying to settle shit down, but I'm not ready. Zoe was great, but after what you said…"

"What *I* said?" Emma interrupted.

"Yeah, when we were at the club and I told you about maybe giving this a try, you said, 'if you're really happy.' I couldn't get that out of my mind. I'm not sure I was really happy. I like to be free, not cuddled up watching some chick flick."

"I didn't mean to mess things up." Emma really felt horrible. If Kyle really liked her and didn't make things between them serious because of something she had joked with him about, she would never forgive herself.

"You didn't. I just wasn't feelin' it. I'm not ready to settle down and get married, and I think that's what she wanted."

Emma was actually thankful that Kyle was using his brain and not his dick. He really needed to find someone better than Zoe, or at least someone who he was truly happy with. "Well, maybe next time you can break up with someone when you are in the same state, or better yet, in person."

"Yeah, kind of a dick move. But if it makes you feel better, I had some chick on top of me when I called her."

Emma gasped. "Are you fucking serious?"

"No," he laughed. "I wanted to see how you'd react."

"God, you're an ass. Oh shit, I gotta go," she said as she heard a knock on the door.

"You headin' to the airport?"

"Yeah, Micah just showed up. He's driving me."

"Have a safe flight. Text me when you get to your mom's. Tell *Monte* I said hello," Kyle joked.

"It's *Micah*," Emma corrected him. "And I will.

151

Later."

"Bye," he said, hanging up. She ran to the door, opening it to see Micah standing there in jeans and a black blazer. His smile made the butterflies flutter around in her stomach.

"Ready?" he asked, leaning up against the door frame.

"Yeah, lemme just grab my bags. Actually...I wanna show you this," Emma said excitedly. She closed her eyes, turned around and reached toward her room. When she opened her eyes, the bags had stopped a few feet away from her. She turned back around to see Micah softly applauding her.

"You're definitely getting better."

"I'm glad you said that, 'cause I've been practicing all morning!"

Micah stepped through the front door, giving her a kiss on the top of her head before he walked over to grab the bags. Emma was sort of hurt that he didn't acknowledge her excitement or anything. She slipped on her jacket, mentally going over everything she had packed so she didn't forget anything. Micah carried the bags down to his SUV while Emma locked up the apartment.

During the drive to the airport, there was an awkward silence between them. She was tempted to ask what was going on, but chickened out each time. When they arrived at Denver International, he finally spoke to her, but only to ask what airline she was on. Emma whispered that it was the East terminal. Since nothing was being said, she assumed he was going to just drop her off at the gate, but instead he drove into the parking garage.

Pulling into a spot, he switched off the engine and she quickly unlatched her seatbelt. Micah grabbed her hand. "Sorry, I didn't mean to be so quiet. A lot of shit is on my mind."

"It's okay," Emma whispered.

They both sat in silence again. Micah continued to act like he was about to say something but then he would run his hands through his thick, black hair. Grabbing both of her hands, he pulled her close and gently kissed her lips.

"I wanted to surprise you," he said as he pulled away. "I'm flying to New York this evening. I wanted to be near you for Christmas."

"Really?" she asked, smiling. She was really impressed by his attempted surprise.

"Yes. I've arranged to have a cocktail party at a smaller club I own out there. I'd love it if you and your mother would come."

"O-okay, that'd be really nice," Emma stuttered.

"I'll help you get your things inside."

She'd only expected to tell her mom about Micah, not actually introduce him. Stepping out of the car, she walked around to help him with her bags. Emma had packed two suitcases full of clothes and shoes. She wasn't used to not having access to all of her things for seven whole days—and a girl could never have too many pairs of shoes. She noticed that Micah had one extra bag along with her things. "Are you bringing your bag?"

"Yeah, I figured I could check in now and hang out with you for a little bit."

"How long until your flight?" Emma asked, shocked that he was willing to hang out until his flight.

"A few hours, but I have some work I can get done."

"Oh. Thanks for coming to keep me company."

"It's my pleasure."

After they checked in their bags, they went through the enormous security line, then grabbed a seat at one of the bars. Prepping for the long flight ahead, they both ordered a beer. Micah suggested they have a nice lunch, so he ordered two steaks as well. Emma told him she wasn't that hungry, but he insisted. She wasn't used to being told what to eat, so she huffed for a few minutes while she sipped on her beer.

As their waiter placed the plates in front of them, Emma couldn't refuse the smell of a filet mignon. They began to eat and Micah started to fill her in on the cocktail party. "So, I planned it for tomorrow night, I hope you don't have any plans."

"I doubt that we'll have any plans, but that's a really far drive for one night."

"That's why I have a private jet arranged to fly you into New York, and I booked a room for you and your mom."

"You did? Wow…I…I don't know what to say, Micah."

"Don't say anything. It'll be a pleasure to have you there."

Emma was more than excited to be invited to the party, but the hard part would be trying to get her mom to go. Emma's mom had always been one to pay for things on her own and she never really accepted help—even when she was raising Emma alone. She didn't even think that her mom dated until Emma was a lot older because she didn't want to have to find someone to babysit. Now that a private plane and room were being given to the two of them, it was going to take some convincing. Finishing the last of her steak, savoring every bite, Emma checked her watch and gasped. "Oh shit! I need to head to my gate! I can't believe I lost track of time!" She stood up and reached for her wallet to grab some cash.

"Don't worry about it, Emma. Go catch your flight. Let me know when you've landed. I may already be en route, but still send me a message."

"Okay, have a safe trip." Emma quickly gave him a kiss, grabbing her purse, and rushed toward her gate.

The attendants were just starting to board the flight when she arrived, trying her hardest to catch her breath. Emma noted to herself: don't eat a big meal and then try to run down half the airport to your gate. She was already a nervous flier, so she should've known better than to eat a meal like that before takeoff. Handing her ticket to the very flamboyant male attendant, Emma walked down the ramp to the plane. She had almost four hours to think of a way to get her mom to New York for tomorrow night. Emma took her seat next to a woman who was around her age and put her headphones on, giving her a slight smile. Quickly taking her phone out of her bag, Emma typed a quick message to her mom.

Emma: Hey, Mom! I've just boarded. On my

way. I love you!

A moment later, she received a message.

Mom: I can't wait to see you, honey. I'll be waiting to pick you up. Love you too!

Tossing her phone back in her bag, Emma flipped through the channels on the in-flight television. The lady next to her picked up her book and began to read. Emma never was one to be social on a plane.

"Good afternoon, ladies and gentlemen. Thank you for flying with us today..." the flight attendant announced over the loud speaker. Emma rested her head back into the leather seat and slowly closed her eyes.

***

"Miss?" the lady sitting next to Emma said, tapping her on the shoulder.

"Huh?" Emma startled awake.

"We landed, everyone is starting to get off."

"Wow, I didn't realize we'd even taken off, let alone landed! Thank you so much for waking me," Emma said, unbuckling her seatbelt and quickly standing up. Everybody had already left as she grabbed her purse, rushing off the plane. As she walked through the terminals, she typed out a text message to Kyle and Micah.

Emma: Landed! Xoxox

After she pressed *send*, Emma looked up to see her mom smiling widely and waving ecstatically. Her mom stood out in a crowd with her flowing brown hair and crystal blue eyes. She was definitely a catch and since she was still young, she was definitely still hot. Emma's mom had her at twenty-three, which to most isn't that young, but it was still weird to think she had her at the age Emma was now.

"Emma! Honey!" she screeched, running up to Emma with open arms. They squeezed each other tightly, and Emma almost didn't want to let her go.

"Hi, Mom, I missed you!" Emma gasped. "I can't breathe, though."

Her mom chuckled, wiping a tear from her eye. "Sorry, honey. I'm just so happy to finally have you home. How was your flight? Oh, you cut your hair! Did you and Kyle make up?"

"Mom, slow down," Emma giggled. "Flight was fine, I actually slept through the entire thing! Do you like my hair? I'm still trying to adjust to it. I only took a few inches off, but it still is a lot to me. And, yeah, Kyle and I are good. We finally got to talk and patched things up. Speaking of which…" Emma pulled her phone out of her bag to see she had two messages.

Kyle: Glad you made it. Tell your mom I said hey, and if she's still single…

Oh my God, he was such a whore. "Kyle says hi," Emma said, quickly closing the message so her mom didn't see the rest.

"Well, tell him hello. I never understood why you two didn't work out. I really like Kyle."

"Yeah, well, he's a great friend. However, he sucks as a boyfriend and I'm not really slut material."

"Slut material?" her mom repeated.

"He likes his girls kinda skanky…I don't know why I'm going into this. Anyway, I gotta talk to you about something."

"Is everything okay?" Her mom stopped, grabbing Emma's arm. "You've called me a couple of times and mentioned weird things. I'm beginning to worry."

"Oh, yeah, I'm fine." Emma grabbed her hand, squeezing it gently. "Let's get out of here. I can tell you on the way home," Emma said, pulling her arm.

Postponing the conversation for the car ride, they walked over to the baggage carousel. Piles of bags were unloaded and crowds of people swarmed around to find their bags. Emma was itching to use her powers to grab her bags, but wanted to avoid using them in public. God only knew how people in an airport would react to seeing someone's bag levitating toward them. Emma shoved her way through, grabbing her bags and walking back to her mom.

"Honey, did you pack enough?" her mom asked sarcastically.

"Nope," Emma laughed. "I didn't know what to wear, so I packed as much as I could." Emma was glad that she narrowed everything down to two bags instead of bringing that third bag.

"You know there's a mall," she said. "So if you

needed something we could always go shopping."

"Oh, I plan on going shopping, but I still wanted to be prepared. It looks beautiful out! Not very typical for December," Emma said, changing the subject.

"I wanted to make sure it was beautiful for you."

"Huh?" Emma's eyes widened and her head darted in her mom's direction.

"I hoped it was going to be beautiful for you." Her mom grabbed one of the bags from Emma's hands and started to walk ahead. Emma quickly caught up to her.

"Oh." Emma was beginning to think she had lost her mind. Did her mom actually say she was making it beautiful for *her*? No, she completely misheard her.

"What did you think I said? Let's get on the road, we're probably going to hit some rush hour traffic." Her mom sighed.

Grabbing the bag back from her mom, Emma walked beside her. She couldn't help but stare at her, wondering if she actually had control over some of the weather. "Wow, when did you get this?" Emma asked, looking at the shiny white Volvo.

"A few months ago. My other car died, so I upgraded. You like?"

"Yeah, super nice!" Emma always loved new car smells, and as she sat down in the passenger seat, she took a deep breath.

"So, what did you want to talk to me about?" her mom asked, starting the car.

Emma really wanted to start the conversation out

with, 'Mom, I have these great powers and I'm super excited and I can't wait to show you,' but she didn't even have the courage to force it out.

"I've started dating a really great guy and he is flying us to New York tomorrow!" Emma blurted.

Chapter Fourteen

"So, I'm just supposed to take a private plane to *New York?*" Emma's mom asked, pacing back and forth. Emma and her mom had been going back and forth on the topic of flying to New York to meet Micah for the last few hours. Emma tried to drop the subject and let her mom cool off, but each time she walked away her mom would bring it up again.

"Mom...it's a small trip. I know you don't like to have things bought for you, but it's more for me! I want you to meet my boyfriend and he's hosting a cocktail party. He wants us there. He's actually *excited* to meet you and you're saying *no?*" Emma could feel her powers beginning to prick at her fingertips. She tried taking a few breaths and concentrate on something soothing.

"Emma Morgan, I'm happy you're happy and you have a boyfriend, but I'm not sure I'm comfortable flying on a private plane to meet a complete stranger. Especially in New York City."

"Grace Adelle," Emma pleaded, "I'm begging you. Please, for once, let go of everything and have a little fun." Emma could see that her mom was beginning to contemplate the idea.

Her mom sighed, taking a seat on the loveseat. Emma walked over and sat next to her, grabbing her hand. "Fine," she whispered.

"Really?" Emma asked excitedly.

"Promise me that you're not dating some member of the mafia or a drug dealer."

"I promise. He owns a nightclub or two," Emma reassured her, hugging her tightly. "Ah! I'm so glad you'll be coming with me! I'm gonna go call him and set up a time. Maybe we can fly out early and do some shopping?" Emma jumped up from the couch and began to dance around.

"That sounds like fun." Her mom smiled up at her. "I'm going to make us some dinner, what can I make you?"

"I'm still kinda full from lunch, so I'll just have something light. Sandwich?"

"Okay, I'll fix us some sandwiches. Let me know what time we need to leave."

"How about *I* make them?" Emma offered, hugging her mom tightly. She nodded into Emma's shoulder, patting her back. Pulling away, Emma ran to her purse. "Let me go call Micah and then I can make them." Emma's phone still had one message from earlier that she had yet to check.

Micah: I'm glad you are safe. I can't wait to taste your beautiful lips again tomorrow night. Xxx

Emma's heart began to race as she reread

Micah's message. She couldn't wait to have his lips on hers again. She dialed his number, hoping he had landed safely.

"Hello, my beauty," Micah answered.

"Hi." She blushed. "How was your flight?"

"Smooth. I'm arriving at the hotel now. Have you spoken to your mom about tomorrow?"

"I have! She's actually in! Well, after hours of arguing about it, she's coming. What time are we supposed to be leaving?"

"Whenever you're ready."

"Great! I was hoping we didn't have a schedule. I'd kinda like to get out there in the morning, so we can do some fun shopping and have some touristy time together."

"I'd like to get my hands on you earlier," he breathed.

"Mmm...I'd like that too," Emma whispered. Just the sound of his voice was turning her on. She wished tomorrow would get here sooner.

"How does nine sound?"

"Really early, but I think we'll manage," Emma sighed.

"I have a meeting with one of my club's managers at ten thirty, but I'll have a car waiting for you."

Emma couldn't believe she was about to actually ask him this, but to reassure her mom it really needed to be asked. "Micah, you aren't a drug dealer or part of the mafia, are you?" she joked, chuckling.

"Where did that come from? But, no, I'm not involved with either."

"Long story, but great. I'll talk to you tomorrow." Emma felt slightly reassured that he wasn't a drug dealer or part of some mafia.

"Sweet dreams."

"Thanks. You too," she sighed, hanging up the phone. With Micah saying things like he wanted his hands on her, she was definitely going to have some sweet dreams.

Emma lay back on her bed, feeling like she was sixteen again after getting off the phone with her crush. She looked around the room, enjoying the walk down memory lane. Her lacrosse stick hung on the wall with her jersey underneath. Emma remembered having to beg her school to let her keep the jersey. There were also little charms hanging around her room. She remembered how her mom loved hanging them around the house when she was growing up. She told her they would protect her. Emma never thought twice about them, but now she was starting to wonder. Her mom startled her with a small knock on the door frame.

"So…what time do we leave tomorrow?" her mom asked.

"It's all on our time, but I thought we could leave about nine-ish to do some shopping, then maybe lunch?"

"That sounds like a great day. And he has a room set up for us as well?"

"Yeah! Mom, don't worry, he's really nice and he's…I really like him."

"You don't think you're rushing things? I'm not trying to be rude, Em. I just fear that you're rushing things with him. You sound almost like me when I met your father."

"Really?" Emma asked quickly sitting up. "I didn't think I was rushing anything. Besides, why are you bringing up my dad?" she snapped.

"I didn't mean to upset you. I'm just trying to play mom for a minute. I'm excited to meet Micah, I promise, I am. As for your dad…never mind."

Emma sighed heavily. She didn't want to have another fight with her mom. "You'll like him. Anyway, let's head downstairs and eat," Emma said, linking her arm through her mom's. They walked downstairs and into the kitchen, where everything looked the same as it did from when Emma was a teenager. It was like a walk down memory lane, looking at all the photographs her mom had framed around the house. There were pictures of Emma throughout the years in school, missing teeth, her senior prom, and even the day she left for college.

Emma made some ham and cheese sandwiches for the both of them and sat down next to her mom at the table. As long as Emma could remember, her mom never wanted to start her day off by reading a sad story in the news, so she would wait until lunch to read the paper.

As they started to finish up, Emma couldn't help but think this would be the best time to ask her mom about what was going on. "Hey, Mom?" Emma asked.

"Uh-huh," she replied, looking over the newspaper.

"I don't even know how to ask this. I'm going to sound completely crazy, but it's killing me." Emma nervously sighed as she began to fidget with her hands.

She looked up. "What's the matter?"

Emma dropped her head. "Do you…I'm finding that I can do…*things.*" Emma waited for a response, her mom telling her she was nuts, but her mom grabbed her hand.

"I know. Honey, maybe we should talk about this." She squeezed Emma's hand and then scooted closer to her.

"I'm sorry, but *what*?" Emma's eyes opened wider, as she was not prepared for her to say she knew this.

Her mom took a deep breath before she started. "You were born with this sort of *talent*, if you wanna call it that. Emma, you're a witch. *I'm* a witch. You were born with powers."

"But if this is something you've known, then why am I just finding out about it?" Emma pulled her hand away from her mom and scooted back a bit. Why would she have hidden this from her?

"I wanted you to live a normal life. I tried to keep you from learning about them and even from trying to use them. I didn't want you to have to explain things to your friends, and most of all, I didn't want to explain it to other parents. The Salem Witch Trials may have taken place a very long time ago, but it doesn't mean people would be more accepting of it now."

"This is insane! I mean that in the greatest way possible, though…but I'm a witch!" Emma jumped up, clapping her hands.

"Emma, it's not something we go around

bragging about. We do still like to keep a lower profile," she said, sitting Emma back down in the chair.

"So, are we part of some sort of coven?" Emma asked.

"No. I'm sorry," she chuckled. "We don't belong to a coven. There really aren't a lot of us out there. We just keep to ourselves and try to keep our secret."

"What if I've already said something?" Emma asked nervously.

"Like to whom?" She sighed.

"Kyle. Well, we thought it was really weird and he was the one who told me to talk to you about it."

"Why would he think that?" Her mom gave her a puzzled look.

"'Cause you own a bookstore and you'd probably know something." Emma laughed.

"Who else did you say something to?"

"Micah," Emma said, cringing.

"Emma! Why would you discuss it with him?" she asked angrily.

"Mom, don't worry! He has powers too!" Emma exclaimed, watching her mom's face change from angry to confused. "He can sense people with powers."

"Really? So, he knew?" her mom asked, puzzled.

"Yeah, so now you really don't have to worry about him. He's kinda one of us." Emma felt like her mom should be more understanding of the situation. She was around someone who understood the meaning of having powers. Emma wasn't sure why her mom was being like this toward Micah.

167

"Well, now I really do have to meet him." She smirked.

"I'm really glad you agreed to go. We'll have some fun," Emma reassured her. They moved from the kitchen into the living room, making themselves comfortable on the couch.

Her mom smiled widely. "Are you all settled in your room?"

"Yeah. It's just weird though."

"Weird?"

"Just seeing everything. It's like I've traveled back in time."

"I was going to pack things away, maybe into the basement, but I like having it around. Especially when I'm missing you." She placed her hand on top of Emma's. Emma did feel bad that she had to go move almost to the other side of the country. It was nice to be home to visit though.

"Aww, I miss you too, Mom." Emma pulled her into a hug, now feeling a little closer to her mom. "So, now that this is all out in the open, I have so many more questions."

"I'll try my best. What would you like to know?"

"How did you suppress my powers?" Emma asked.

"When you were younger, you…well, I just tried to raise you without any sort of powers. I even tried my hardest not to use my powers around you."

"What are your powers?" This, by far, was the coolest and weirdest conversation that Emma and her mom ever had.

"I'm a healer. So, when you were young and I couldn't use my powers to heal that scraped knee or when you broke your arm in middle school, it was the hardest thing ever. I just didn't want to have you confused by everything or have your friends act weird."

"Wow. This is really cool. I'm a witch." Emma couldn't believe she was actually a witch.

Her mom chuckled.

"Did...er...did my dad have powers." Emma asked hesitantly.

"He did, but let's not talk about that." She sighed.

"Oh. Okay." Emma really didn't care if her dad had any powers, but it was really great to know that she wasn't going crazy. She was a witch.

***

"Oh yes! Right there! Fuck yes!" he bellowed.

"That was intense!" Emma breathed.

"You're fucking amazing. I can't get enough of you, Emma." Micah rolled her off him and lay beside her. He grabbed her hand, individually kissing each finger.

"Let's go again?" Emma asked, smiling cheekily.

"I'd love to, but this is where we end."

"What?" Emma jolted up.

"You're gonna die, and I don't know how I'm supposed to save you."

Tears began to stream down her face. "I'm going to die?"

"I don't know."

"I'm so confused! What are you saying?"

169

"Emma Morgan, I love…"

Emma quickly sat up in bed, drenched in sweat. Her nerves were rattled and she felt like she had been crying for hours. The clock read seven thirty in the morning, and thankfully, she had to wake up, as she couldn't imagine having to relive that dream. Or nightmare.

Grabbing her toiletries out of her bag, Emma crept down the hall to the shower. Her mom's door was shut, so if she was still catching the last bit of sleep, Emma didn't want to wake her. Taking a quick, lukewarm shower, so she didn't take all the hot water, Emma hurried to get ready. The smell of coffee lured her out of the bathroom. She postponed putting her makeup on until she grabbed a hot cup.

"Morning," her mom greeted her as Emma entered the kitchen. Her mom was sitting at the table with her legs pulled up to her chest. As far back as she could remember, her mom would always sit like this and drink her coffee.

"Hey, how long have you been up?" Emma asked, pouring coffee into a mug. Emma took a seat next to her at the table.

"A little bit. You sleep okay?"

"I did," Emma lied. "It was a little weird to be in the same sheets as senior year, though."

"I wash them, so dust doesn't collect on them. I remember when we bought them."

"Me too. I *had* to have them."

"I was surprised you wanted sheets with elephants on them, but you bought them." They both laughed, sipping on their coffee. Emma went through a phase where she was obsessed with elephants, and now looking back, it was a little silly.

"Well, I just need to finish up my makeup and then we can go, I mean, if you're ready."

"Yeah, I'm packed and showered. Take your time."

"I really do appreciate you doing this for me," Emma said sincerely.

"I know. I'm happy to do this for you." She squeezed Emma's hand. "This will be fun! Oh, look! It's snowing!"

Looking out the window, a soft snow began to fall. It looked so beautiful. They finished their coffee, watching the lawn collect a dusting of snow.

"All right, I'm gonna fix my makeup. I'll be ready in fifteen minutes. Sound good?" Emma asked, placing her cup in the sink.

"I'll be waiting for you down here. Hopefully the snow lets up."

"I hope so too. I don't want to have to fly in snow."

Emma's mom gave her a quick hug before she left the kitchen. Emma ran upstairs into the bathroom and finished up her hair and makeup, then picked out some clothes and shoved them into a small overnight bag she had stored in her closet. She was so excited to see Micah that she didn't really pay attention to what she was packing. Like her mom had said, if she forgot something, they'd be doing shopping anyway.

"I'm ready!" Emma said, running down the stairs. Her mom grabbed her overnight bag and keys off the couch and followed Emma out the front door. Overcome with excitement, Emma almost didn't notice the snow had stopped. "Oh, wow! Look, it stopped snowing! The sun looks like it's trying to push its way through the clouds."

"We really lucked out!"

"Yeah. We did."

"Let's go shopping, what do ya say?"

"I say, uhh *yes!*" Emma giggled. She'd never been to New York City, so she was overwhelmed with excitement.

Her mom started the car and they made their way to the airport.

***

When they pulled into the private lot, Emma became a little nervous. She'd never flown in anything smaller than a commercial airliner. The plane waiting for them was only made for a maximum of six people, and that included the pilot. Her mom wrapped her arm around her, silently reassuring Emma they'd be okay.

"Good morning, ladies," a gray haired man greeted them. "I'm Connor. I'll be taking you to New York City this morning."

"Morning, Connor," Emma's mom responded with a smile.

"Hi," Emma said nervously.

"I want to reassure you, I've flown for twenty-seven years in all conditions and yes, I've crash landed before. I'm prepared for everything and anything."

Not really the words Emma was looking for him

172

to say to her, but it did put a little comfort to the swirling butterflies in her stomach. They all boarded the plane and Emma tightened her seatbelt several times as Connor rolled them down the runway. Emma grabbed her mom's hand tightly as they ascended from the ground. Thankfully, it was only a forty minute flight.

The little bit of turbulence they had quickly passed, and before Emma knew it they were approaching the runway. As they stepped off the plane, the New York air was frigid. A town car was waiting for them with a driver standing by the back passenger door. Emma's mom and Connor stood by the plane, chatting, as Emma rushed into the car and out of the cold. Emma watched as her mom walked toward her, grinning from ear to ear.

"Well, someone is obviously happy." Emma laughed. Her mom pretended she didn't hear her. "So, I'll take that as a yes. Are you up for some breakfast and then a day of shopping—just you and me?"

"Yes! That sounds great! When do I get to meet this new boyfriend, Micah?"

"Lemme see!" Emma said, smiling brightly. Pulling out her phone, she quickly typed out a text.

Emma: Hi! We've landed and we're heading into the city. Would you like to meet for breakfast?

"Ladies, where can I take you," the driver asked, pulling out of the lot.

"Ummm. Fifth Avenue?" Emma suggested. She

looked at her mom, who was shrugging her shoulders.

"Fifth it is," the driver agreed, speeding down the highway.

Emma's phone buzzed with an incoming text.

Micah: Sorry, love. I need to head into a meeting, but I'll meet you later for lunch.

"Micah has a business meeting to attend to, but said he'll meet us later. So it's just us girls for the day!" Emma told her mom, placing her phone into her purse. What a great day to spend with her mom—in New York City. They grabbed a quick bite to eat before walking through what seemed like every store. Emma couldn't believe how much money they were spending. "Where to next?" Emma asked, sorting the bags she was carrying.

"Someplace to sit down. My feet are beginning to hurt!"

"Lunch?" Emma asked, checking her watch.

Her mom nodded, linking her arm with Emma's. They started to walk to a nearby café when Emma's phone began to ring. She pulled it out of her purse with her free hand and saw Micah's number flashing on the screen. Showing her mom, smiling widely, Emma quickly answered it.

"Hi!"

"Hey, beautiful. How are you ladies enjoying your time in the big city?" he replied. His voice was so sexy.

"We're having a great time! Shopping a little too much, but still having fun. We're on our way to lunch. Can you take a lunch break?"

"As a matter of fact, I was just on my way out to grab a bite. I'd love to meet you."

"Great! Any suggestions?"

"Where are you ladies now?"

I looked around for the nearest street signs. "I think Eighth," Emma said, looking at her mom who was shrugging her shoulders at her.

"Okay, there should be a diner on the corner. There should be a sign with a horse on the side, I'll be there in about ten minutes." He instructed a driver where to go.

"We'll see you soon," Emma said, hanging up. She put her phone back into her bag and turned to her mom. "We're heading to a diner with a horse sign. He'll meet us there in ten minutes." They organized their bags in their hands and walked to the end of the block to see a sign that read *'Dark Horse Tavern'*. Emma held the door open for her mom as they walked in from the chilly December air.

"Hi ladies, two for lunch?" the hostess asked, grabbing two menus.

"Actually, three. He'll be here in a few minutes," Emma added. The hostess grabbed an extra menu before leading them to a table. The hardwood floors creaked under their feet as they arrived at their round table. They both placed their bags in the corner and removed their jackets as the hostess set the menus down on the table.

"Chloe will be your waitress today. Enjoy." She smiled and skipped toward the front of the restaurant.

"Is it just me, or is the hostess a little *too* perky?" Emma joked.

"I definitely think she's had way too much of something." Her mom laughed.

As Chloe brought some water, they browsed over the menu. Everything at this point looked delicious, so much that her stomach growled loudly and Emma's mom heard it, making them both giggle. Emma tried to decide between a sandwich and salad as goose bumps ran down her arms. She could hear his voice talking to the hostess. Emma's heart began to flutter.

Micah strode across the room to the table. His black hair was slicked back, dark eyes gleaming in the sunlight which poured in through the ten foot windows. He looked irresistible.

"Hi, beautiful." Micah greeted her with a kiss to her cheek. His lips were cold, but felt so good against her blushed cheeks.

"Hey. Micah, I'd like to introduce you to my mom, Grace."

Her mom stood, holding her hand out to Micah. "Pleased to meet you, Micah. My daughter has talked about you non-stop."

Emma's face blushed again. "Thanks for embarrassing me, Mom."

"Well, Mrs.—" Micah reached out and shook her hand.

"Please, just call me Grace." She smiled.

"Grace, it is great to meet you as well. I now know where Emma gets her beauty from."

"That is very sweet of you, Micah. Please come sit down, we're both starving." Grace scooted her chair over to give Micah a bit more room on the other side of Emma.

"Thanks, Grace. The food here is to die for. I've had just about everything here. I'm a big fan of their fish and chips."

"That does sound good, I might try that as well," Grace said, glancing once more at the menu.

Emma was so happy to see her mom taking a liking to Micah.

Chapter Fifteen

Once they finished lunch, Micah had to head out for another meeting, but after a day of shopping, spending a lot of money, and looking at the beautiful sights around the city, Emma and her mom were more than happy to arrive at the hotel. Emma was glad her mom was able to meet Micah before the cocktail party.

"I don't know how I'm going to wear heels!" Emma whined, rubbing her feet.

"Why don't you go take a long bath and relax them?" her mom suggested, laying her dress out on the bed.

"You know, that doesn't sound bad at all," Emma said, walking into the bathroom. "Oh my God! Have you *seen* the tub in here?" Her mom chuckled as Emma peeked around the corner. Emma closed the door, noticing tea candles lining the counter and without any hesitation, she snapped her fingers, lighting each one.

The water was incredibly warm as Emma sank into the tub, and her mind slowly drifted to dirty thoughts of Micah and her...in that very tub. Oh, the things she could do with him. Her fingers slowly caressed their way down her abdomen.

Just as Emma was about to slide her fingers between her legs, Emma's mom knocked on the door. "Emma, honey, would you like anything from room service? I think I'm going to order something small."

Emma sighed, bringing her fingers back to the surface. "Yeah, I'll split an appetizer with you. I'll be out in a minute." So much for helping herself out.

As she dried off, Emma heard her mom ordering some calamari and prawn cocktail. Her stomach began to rumble, so maybe it was a good idea she was ordering some food. While they were out today, she wasn't able to find a dress she liked, so she went the skirt route. Even going for something a little risqué, Emma bought a garter belt and some thigh-high stockings. She quickly dressed in the bathroom.

"Oh! You look beautiful! I really love that skirt!" her mom exclaimed.

"Thanks. You don't think I'm going to be underdressed?" Emma asked, smoothing out the skirt.

"No, I think it's just right."

Their food arrived a few moments later and they had a mini picnic on one of the beds while they watched *The Notebook*. It was so nice to have a 'younger' mom, especially since she could appreciate Ryan Gosling just as much as she did.

"What time should we head out?" her mom

asked, taking one last bite of calamari.

"He told me nine, earlier." Emma wiped her mouth and placed her napkin on the plate.

"Well, it's eight thirty. Shall we make our way down?"

Emma nodded, straightening her skirt. Slipping on her heels and coat, they made their way down to the lobby. The club was only a block away, so they decided to brave the cold. As they approached the building, Emma noticed Connor was bundled up, waiting by the entrance. Her mom smiled and gave him a nonchalant wave. They walked up to the front door where a muscular guy covered in tattoos was sitting.

"This is a private party," he said, holding up his hand.

"Um, we're guests of Micah Oliver," Emma said, pointing to the clipboard.

"I'm sorry. You must be…Emma and Mrs.…."

"Grace, please," her mom interrupted. The guy didn't even acknowledge Connor.

"Grace," he repeated. "Please go inside. Mr. Oliver is expecting you in the main room." The man opened the door for them and they hurried in to escape the cold.

Micah was on his phone, pacing back and forth as they entered the lobby. Emma could hear him getting frustrated with the person on the other line. "Look, she's here. No! I'll…" He began to whisper as Emma came closer. "She's not quite ready yet…I know that's what you want…I'll call you later, I want to discuss something more with you." He hung up with his call and greeted them. "You look beautiful," Micah whispered in Emma's ear, leading her into the room. Emma's mom was not far behind as she chatted with Connor.

"Thank you," Emma said, smiling. "Everything okay?"

He nodded. "Grace, it's so nice to see you, again."

"Thank you, Micah. It's very nice to see you too. This is a really nice club. Emma said you *own* this?"

"I do. This was my first business I started up," he said, smiling as he guided them through the lobby. "Connor, it's nice to see you," Micah said, shaking his hand.

As they entered the dimly lit main room, there were about twenty people scattered around, sitting on the dark couches. There were curtains hanging from the ceiling and candles were spread out throughout the club. This was definitely a place Emma would love to hang out in. Emma thought Kyle would get a kick out of this place too. Micah excused himself from Emma's side to greet a couple seated on one of the couches. Emma walked back to her mom, who was waiting for Connor to get her a drink. "Everything okay?" Emma asked her.

"Yeah." She smiled. "Connor was just telling me that he'd booked us reservations at a nice Italian restaurant tonight."

"Oh, you're leaving?" Emma sulked.

"I'll probably stay for a drink or two, and then I might let you two have some fun."

"Are you sure? I'd love to have you here!"

"Yeah, I'm sure," her mom replied, nodding.

They walked over to an empty couch, taking a seat as they waited for Micah and Connor to return.

"So, Connor, huh?" Emma joked.

"He seems like a very kind man. We exchanged numbers as we got off the plane."

"Way to go, Mom!" Emma giggled. She was really proud of her mom putting herself out there.

"Grace, are you doing okay?" Micah asked, placing his arm on Grace's shoulder.

"I'm fine, Micah. Thank you. However, I was just telling Emma that Connor and I have some dinner plans for later, so we'll be only staying for a drink or two and then heading out."

"I'd hate to see you leave, but I understand."

Connor returned to Grace's side, handing her a glass of merlot. Emma's mom thanked him and began to carry on a conversation. Micah took a seat next to Emma.

"So, you own this club?" Emma asked.

"I do. I have thought about selling it, but I love to come back to New York every once in a while and tend to end up here."

"I love it. It suits you."

"How so?" he asked.

"It's dark, but sexy." Emma winked at Micah.

Micah smiled, kissing her hand. "Can I get you a drink?"

"I'd love some white wine."

"I'll be back in a moment."

Emma watched the other guests mingle as she waited for Micah to return. Her mom was laughing and seemed to be having a great time with Connor. Another couple caught her eye in another section, both were dressed in all black. The man was blond and he looked as if he were in his forties. Beside him was a younger woman, she was obviously much younger than he. She had her fire-red hair tightly pulled back into a bun. They were cuddled up on the couch, flirting and lightly kissing each other. Micah reappeared, handing her a wine glass.

"Umm, I'm gonna feel silly for asking, but who are all these people?" Emma whispered.

"Just some old friends of mine. A lot of them are regulars at the club and around the holidays, they seem to hang out here more. I thought about closing it to make it more of a private event, but some of them don't have family and this is like home to them."

"Oh, seriously? I think that's very sweet of you. I'm glad you kept it open."

"Emma," her mom interrupted. "I think Connor and I are going to head out."

"Already?" Emma whined. They just got there and Emma thought it was a little rude that her mom was already heading out.

"Yeah, but you stay and have fun. I'll see you back at the hotel."

"Grace, will you stay for one dance?" Micah asked, standing up and holding his hand out.

"Umm," her mom hesitated, looking at Connor.

"Go ahead, I'll finish my drink and then we can go," Connor said, holding up his scotch.

Emma's mom nodded and took Micah's hand as he led her to a small dance floor over by the bar. Emma thought this would be a good opportunity to get to know Connor. "Connor, how long have you been flying again?"

"For about twenty-seven years now. So yes, I'm a bit older than your mom."

"Oh, I'm not worried about that." Emma smiled. "Where are you guys going to eat?"

"There's a wonderful European restaurant on the Upper East Side."

"Sounds delicious. I'm glad you two have hit it off." Emma observed Connor as he smiled while he watched her mom on the dance floor. Emma turned to face them, but her mom's smile began to fade into a frown as Micah whispered into her ear. Emma could hear bits and pieces of what Micah was saying.

"I know about her powers," he whispered. Emma immediately blushed. She couldn't believe Micah was telling her mom that he knew. Emma could've heard it wrong, so she sat still and continued to listen to Connor talk about his flying experiences.

Grace slowly pulled away, then Micah kissed her knuckles before he led her back to the couch. Connor quickly stood, setting his glass on the end table.

"All right, Emma, I'll see you later. Connor, you ready?" her mom asked.

"Grace, Connor, thank you for coming tonight," Micah said.

"Micah," her mom responded coldly. "Bye, sweetie," she said, kissing Emma's cheek. She hooked arms with Connor and they made their way out of the club.

"Is she okay?" Emma asked Micah.

"Yeah, why do you ask?"

"She looked a little upset on the dance floor."

"I wasn't aware. Would you care to dance?" Emma noticed that he quickly changed the subject, but she also didn't know if she was just imagining the situation.

"I'd like that." Emma took his hand and walked with him onto the dance floor.

The club played soft, sensual music. She loved how close they were, feeling every part of his body touching hers. His hand softly moved up and down her back. His other hand crept up her leg, feeling the strap of her garter belt. He pulled away, looking at bit surprised. "Thigh-highs?"

Emma nodded, slightly blushing.

"Come," he ordered, pulling her by the hand into a back room that was behind the bar. It looked as if it was a warehouse, where the bar received its deliveries. Emma's heart was about to explode out of her chest. "You've been on my mind all day and now, I can't wait to have you."

"Here?" she asked, looking around.

"Yes, here." Micah grabbed a hold of her, laying her gently on the ground. "Tell me what you want," he breathed.

"You," she moaned as he kissed every inch of her leg, lifting it in the air. He looked at her intensely before ripping off her sweater. Her breathing hitched. "Only you."

He slid her panties down her legs, throwing them off to the side. "Emma, you're all I want."

Micah quickly unbuttoned his black slacks, shoving them down. He slowly pushed into her, pinning her arms above her head. Every time she tried to pull her arms away, he pushed harder into her. Emma began to feel her powers building at her fingers. "That's it, Emma, let the darkness in," Micah groaned.

With each thrust into her, she could feel some sort of darkness overwhelming her. It felt…incredible.

***

Soon after Micah and Emma had left the club, they ended up in his room. She couldn't tell if it was the few drinks she had or the dark feeling that overwhelmed her that was the reason she didn't remember leaving. Either way, lying in his arms felt amazing. "You okay?" he whispered. Emma slowly nodded as she started to fall asleep.

For the first time in the last few weeks, her dreams didn't seem to bother her. In fact, they were rather…peaceful. Unfortunately, Emma was awakened by the sound of her phone ringing. She tried not to wake Micah, sliding out of his arms to grab her phone.

"Hello?" Emma whispered, sneaking out of the room and walking into the living room.

"Emma, where are you? I've been up most of the night worried sick about you!" her mom shouted on the other line.

"What time is it?"

"Seven!"

"Jesus! I'm so sorry, Mom. I didn't even realize I'd slept that long. I'm in the hotel, I'll be down there in a few minutes."

"Damn straight. I'm ready to head home."

"What? Mom, come on! I'd like to have breakfast with Micah before we leave."

"Emma...I...fine."

"What's the matter?" Emma was beginning to feel a little hurt by her mom's sudden change of attitude. She really thought her mom liked Micah, but now she was rushing Emma off.

"Nothing. I guess I'm a little tired."

"Okay, let me wake him up and then I'll be down. We can go have some breakfast and then fly home," Emma scoffed.

"All right," her mom sighed.

Emma hung up the phone and made her way back into the bedroom. Micah was wide awake, propped up on a pillow, smiling at her.

"Morning, sorry if I woke you," Emma greeted, smiling back.

"Morning. I only woke because I didn't have you in my arms."

"Well, I worried my mom and she's a little pissed. Okay, a lot pissed. Would you mind coming to breakfast with us?" Emma asked, feeling a little ridiculous that her mom was acting this way.

"I don't mind at all. The restaurant downstairs serves the best breakfast."

"Perfect. I'm gonna go reassure my mom that I'm fine and we'll meet you in a half hour?"

Emma leaned in and kissed Micah. "Umm...can I use your shirt? Since my sweater is still ripped..."

"I guess I got carried away," he chuckled.

"Just a little. I don't remember, really, getting back to the hotel. Please say I didn't wander around

New York City with a ripped sweater."

"No, you wore my blazer underneath your coat."

"Just making sure. Mind if I ask *how* we got here?" Emma quickly buttoned up his white dress shirt and grabbed her things.

"We walked, well you for a little bit. I carried you the rest of the way."

"I'm so sorry." Emma still tried to recall the last part of the evening, but nothing was coming to mind.

"Don't be. I rather enjoyed it." He smiled devilishly. That smile was going to get Emma in trouble, and if she were to stay any longer, she would make her mom even more pissed at her. Besides, starving was an understatement. Emma waved goodbye, blowing him one last kiss, and then rushed out of the room.

Thankfully, Emma was on the same floor as the room Micah had booked for her. She didn't have to wait for any elevators or climb any stairs. Instead, she dashed toward her room and fumbled with the door key. Her mom was sitting on the edge of the bed, flipping through channels. "I'm really sorry," Emma mumbled.

"We'll talk about this later. Go get showered so we can go eat."

"Are you going to be pissed off at me the rest of the trip?" Emma snapped.

"Am I not supposed to be?"

"No, Mom, you're not. I'm an adult and if I want to spend the night with my boyfriend, I sure as hell can."

"A phone call, Emma, that's all I would've liked.

We're in a big city and God knows what could've happened." Her mom threw her arms in the air, standing up. Emma felt like she was in high school all over again.

"Geez, okay. I should've called!" Emma shouted.

"Just go shower," her mom demanded.

Emma rolled her eyes, walking into the bathroom. The warm water felt so relaxing. She could've stayed in the shower longer, but heaven forbid she make her mom wait for her any longer. Since she wasn't around to see, she started to use her powers to help her get ready.

"You ready?" Emma asked as she stepped out of the bathroom.

"That was quick!" her mom stated, looking at her watch.

"I call it 'the college shower,'" Emma joked. She was still annoyed with her little attitude toward her, but she didn't want to ruin breakfast with Micah.

"The college shower?" Her mom laughed.

"Yeah, when you're really late for your morning class but you still want to take a shower, you learn how to haul ass."

Her mom chuckled. At least she was loosening up. "Grab your purse and let's go eat."

Shoving her phone in her pocket, Emma grabbed her wallet and they headed for the lobby. As the two of them exited the elevators, the lobby was glistening with Christmas lights and a group of carolers were singing along with a pianist. Christmas was in a couple of days. Sitting in one of the lobby chairs, Micah was dressed in a tight black t-shirt and blue jeans. As he stood up, every dirty thought Emma had ever had about him ran through her mind.

"Good morning, Grace. I'm sorry to have kept Emma away last night."

"Micah." Grace nodded. "I told Emma already, but next time…a phone call would be nice."

"I understand. How about some breakfast? Connor tells me that you two really hit it off. Have you already arranged a flight time?"

"Pardon?" her mom asked.

"Connor. I try to book flights with him as he's an excellent pilot. Anyway, he said that he'd already spoken to you."

"Yes, we did talk earlier. I set up a departure time already, thank you." Grace really seemed to be snappy toward Micah. Emma began to feel a little upset with the way her mom was acting.

"Who's hungry?" Emma chimed in. Micah and her mom both smiled at her and began to walk to an open booth. Emma was torn on which side she was to take. Sit with her mom? Or sit with Micah. Thankfully, as Emma was about to take a seat, Connor walked in.

"Connor!" her mom said happily.

"Will you be joining us?" Micah offered.

"I'd love to. I was here because when I spoke to Grace, she said that she was ready to leave at eight. The traffic was horrendous to get through, though."

"Here, you can sit with my mom!" Emma offered, sitting next to Micah. "Everything looks way too good," Emma said as she looked over the menu. She couldn't help but see her mom looking up at Micah with such disapproval. Now, more than ever, she couldn't wait to have this talk with her mom.

·

Chapter Sixteen

After everyone finished their meals, Connor suggested they start to head out, since a storm was expected to be blowing in later that afternoon. Grace agreed, and Connor went back to the room to gather the last of her and Emma's things.

"I don't want to leave," Emma whined, hugging Micah.

"Then stay."

"I don't think that'd go over so well with her. I think she's still a little pissed off about me not being back in the room."

"You're an adult, Emma."

"Yes, I know. But I *am* supposed to be spending this time with her."

"How about I come visit you?" Micah suggested.

"You'd come visit me?" Emma asked excitedly.

"Of course. Is there someplace we could meet?"

"There's a beautiful park I used to hang out in high school. The trees are all lit up around Christmas, it's magnificent. Are you seriously coming out to see me?"

"Text me the place and I'll be there. I really want to see you." Emma nodded as he pulled her into a passionate kiss.

As they broke away, Emma's mom stood with their bags in the lounge, impatiently checking her watch. "I'd better go," Emma whispered.

"I'll see you soon, then." Micah opened the door for Emma and her mom as they walked out of the hotel lobby. Waving one last time to Micah, they followed Connor to the town car that was parked outside. There was a silence between them as they traveled to the airport. Emma couldn't *wait* to hear what her mom had to say.

"Are we going to talk or are you going to stay mad at me for the rest of the way home?" Emma asked her mom as they began to board the plane.

"I'd rather it waited until we were home."

"Great, another hour of silence. This will be a *fantastic* time," Emma grumbled.

"Emma? What is with you?" she snapped.

"Me? What's with *me*? Have you ever considered the fact that I saw the way you were glaring at Micah during breakfast, you left the party early…"

Her mom interrupted, "Party? It was *hardly* a party. There was hardly anyone there and…it was nothing. He was showing off for you, Emma."

"Be that as it may, he wanted to have us there so he could get to know you!" Emma shouted.

"Emma, let's discuss this more after we get home." She sighed, leaning back in her seat.

"'Cause we don't want to embarrass *you* in front of your new boyfriend?" Emma pointed to the cockpit. "It's funny, I didn't want you to embarrass me in front of the guy I'm seeing, but you couldn't care less. Now that it's *you*…"

Her mom began to tear up as the plane took off. Emma knew there was definitely something darker about herself. She would never have talked to her mother like that before. It felt empowering to put her mom beneath her.

They didn't speak for the rest of the flight, and Emma didn't even say goodbye to Connor as they left the plane. Emma went straight to the car and waited for her mom to arrive. Emma was half-tempted to make her mom fall on her face as she made her way to the car, but she didn't want to listen to her mom complain or bitch at her anymore.

Emma fiddled with her bracelet as her mom began to drive the car. "Where'd you get that?" she asked, holding up Emma's wrist.

"Micah gave it to me. Why?" Emma asked, pulling her hand away from her mom's grip.

"Take it off!" she commanded.

"Excuse me?" Emma snapped. "So, because you don't like him, I'm not allowed to wear his gifts?"

"This one especially!" she shouted.

"Whatever, Mom." Emma rolled her eyes and leaned her head back. They had a little bit of a drive and she couldn't wait to be home.

Once they pulled into the driveway, Emma grabbed her bags and quickly ran inside. Her mom was close behind. "Emma! Give me the bracelet," she demanded.

"I'm not giving you *my* bracelet. Maybe Connor can get you one!" Emma screamed.

She reached over and grabbed Emma's wrist. Emma used a little bit of power to push her away. A shocked look washed over her face. Suddenly, her wrist swished and the bracelet went flying off of Emma's wrist and across the room, crystals flying everywhere. Emma dropped to the ground, tears rolling down her cheeks as she tried to pick the beads up.

"I'm sorry, honey...but..." her mom began.

"Don't!" Emma shouted, throwing the beads on the ground and running toward her room. Slamming the door behind her, she threw herself onto the bed and began to cry harder. Emma felt devastated that her mom could just destroy a gift of hers.

***

"Emma? Can you open the door? We really need to talk. *Please*," her mom begged, tapping at the door. Emma wiped the tears from her eyes, waving her hand to open the door. "May I come in?" she asked, peeking her head in.

"I guess," Emma sighed. "Look, I get it. You don't like Micah. I'm not a little girl anymore, so you can't forbid me from seeing someone."

"I know. So, I'm going to tell you the whole story and let you choose for yourself."

"The whole story?" Emma asked, confused.

"Yes. The whole story." Her mom took a seat on the edge of the bed. "Emma, I know you're learning all these powers. But, you don't just have a little power."

"What do you mean?"

"I mean, you can do a lot more than you realize. You were born with a lot of powers and you used to be able to do so many good things. But…" Her eyes began to water and she took a deep breath before trying to continue, "Your father tried to hurt you. He *did* hurt you. You don't remember because I wanted to keep this memory from you, so I placed a small spell on you so you wouldn't remember."

"What happened?" Emma asked, sitting up, grabbing her mom's hand.

"Emma, each witch is born with a certain sort of power. You can improve that power and maybe learn how to perfect it. You can learn how to do other things, but you won't be able to truly master it. It takes almost a lifetime to really get to know that new power. I've been blessed with having a couple of powers, my parents were very strong. I can have a say on the weather and I'm a healer." She paused a moment and ran her fingers through her hair. "Your father…he's very strong too. We met through our parents. As we began to get more serious, my parents tried to warn me about him. My mother could actually see glimpses of the future, and she told me he was going to turn dark. I didn't want to believe her, even though everything she ever saw was true. I was young and in love. Later that year, they mysteriously died. Your father was so consoling and promised he would take care of me. We were soon married and found a nice apartment in New York City. You were conceived not long after that and I thought my life was going to get so much better. When you were born, my grandmother told me she could sense how strong you were right away, that your powers would be stronger than anyone's in the family."

"So, you're saying that my powers are stronger than yours?" Emma questioned. She couldn't believe she had more powers than she realized. Let alone stronger powers than her whole family.

"Yes. Unfortunately, your father was furious. He had studied night and day to become stronger and here you were, a newborn, and had already exceeded his powers. I began to notice changes in him over the next few years. It wasn't a sudden change, but he slowly began to fade away. He didn't want to be around us and he would stay in the basement practicing and studying. He would even sleep down there. I never thought he'd do anything. One day when you were little, you'd come home from school and I had gone to the store. Your dad was at home, so I didn't think I'd have to be too worried. I'd forgotten my wallet and I found…" Her mom began to cry.

"Mom, what happened?" Emma asked, grabbing her hands.

"I should've just taken you with me…" She sniffed.

"You said it yourself, you didn't think he'd do anything to harm me," Emma reassured.

"You're right, I didn't. I came home and I could feel the dark energy surrounding the house. I saw your backpack and homework on the floor, scattered about. I called out for you, but when you didn't answer, I began to panic. I ran downstairs to find your dad and he was trying a spell…he was trying to remove your powers from you. I'd heard about this spell, but it was so dark and almost forbidden. He was trying to conjure it...on you!"

"What happened?"

"He wasn't successful, obviously. He almost killed you, though! I hit him with a shovel and he fell to the ground. I then grabbed you and ran. I didn't know where I was going, but I ran. Since I'm a healer and I caught it in time, there was no real damage. You were just very weak. I ended up moving in with another witch friend and she was able to take the memory away from you. I didn't want you to have to relive any of that. We moved to Ipswich because it was big enough to hide us, but small enough that I could have some people look out for us."

"I don't even know what to say..." Emma shook her head in disbelief.

"You don't have to say anything. I know I should've told you sooner, but I thought if you didn't know...you could live a normal life. I wanted you safe and protected. Somehow your powers were triggered and you had to find out the wrong way."

"It was really strange, they were triggered the day after I met Micah."

"Emma, don't get mad, but I think that your father is still looking for you. I think he may have sent Micah."

"No! Micah has done nothing but help me!" Emma snapped.

"Emma, that bracelet...where'd he get it?" she asked quietly.

"A shop in Denver. Umm...La Bella Morte."

"Ying?"

"Yeah...how'd you know?" Emma asked, surprised.

"Ying, she's dark. She makes beautiful jewelry, but she casts dark magic on them, and they almost possess a person. She used to work with your father."

"I see," Emma said, hanging her head. Micah had known Ying, and he had the bracelet made for her.

"I know you like him, Emma, but I think there's something more to him."

"So you think that he's been sent to kill me or something?"

"Micah is dark. When we were on the dance floor he started to go on about how he knew about your powers and how he wanted to help you. I didn't want to hear any more of it, so that's why I left. I didn't want to argue with him in the middle of his party. I think he's been sent to find you by your father, and he's not a man who gives up. If he has truly become dark, and with the powers that you possess, he's going to stop at nothing to make sure you're not around."

"Mom, that's kinda morbid..."

"Honey, you don't know your father."

"So, what *are* my powers?"

"You're what we call a white witch. You possess every power. You can heal, see glimpses of the future, change the weather, and that's just the start. You name it, you've got it."

"And my dad wants me dead for them?" Emma couldn't believe that she was asking if her dad would possibly kill her. Her own father!

"He thinks he can take your powers from you. He just cannot bear the thought of you being able to outdo him."

"Do you think he killed your parents?"

"I don't doubt it," she said, hanging her head.

"Great. And he's my dad. Is that why you hung all those trinkets around my room? You said they would protect me."

"I'm sorry, honey. Sebastian Blackwood was so charming and endearing when we were first married. As for the trinkets, yes, that is exactly why I hung them. They're protection charms. I tried to keep you safe any way I could. I still want to keep you as safe as possible."

"I know you do, Mom. I know. So, this is going to sound weird…"

"What?" her mom panicked.

"I don't know why I'm suddenly thinking of this, but Micah said his bartender has powers as well. Can you, I mean, is it possible to make a drink that will make a person sick and then forget about it?" Emma began to wonder if Micah really did have something to do with Kyle getting sick during Micah's club opening night.

"I'm sure there is. Why? Do you think it happened to you?"

"No. Kyle."

"When did this happen?"

"A couple weeks ago. We were at Micah's grand opening and he was fine and then had to go home 'cause he was really sick. When I got home, he didn't remember any of it and felt fine."

"I don't doubt some magic was used on him."

"Mom, I'm going to need your help," Emma said, combing her fingers through her hair.

"With what?" her mom asked curiously.

"Well, first, I kinda lost my job. Second, I need your help to get stronger. I don't want to live another day having to worry if my dad is going to hurt me."

"You lost your job? What happened?"

"Well, I kind of had a dark moment and lost it on this dick that worked there. I actually quit in a really bad way. Micah helped clear it up, but I told them I couldn't work there anymore."

"Emma…" She sighed. "Are you staying here, then?" Her face lit up with excitement.

"Sorry, I'm not. I'm going to need as much help as I can get before I go home. I have a feeling I need to be back at my home."

Grace nodded her head and stood up. "We'll begin in the morning. We have five days and we're going to need every minute of it. As for a job, I'm sure you'll find one. Until then, I can give you some money."

As Emma stood from the bed, her mom pulled her into her, squeezing tightly. "I love you, Mom."

"I love you too. Get some sleep." Her mom began to walk out of the room.

"I actually need to see Micah."

"Emma," she sighed. "I thought we discussed this?" she said, stopping in the doorway.

"We did. Don't worry, I'll be back real soon," Emma promised.

"Be careful," she said, kissing Emma's head.

Grabbing her coat and purse, her mom followed

Emma down the stairs. Her mom handed her the car key as she headed for the front door. As Emma started the car and waited for it to warm up, she pulled out her phone and called Micah. After two rings, he answered, "Hey. Are you able to meet me now?"

"Yeah, I'm on my way. I'll meet you at the park."

"I can't wait to see you," he purred into the phone.

"See you in a few." Emma ended the call and backed out of the driveway, driving the few miles to the park they had agreed to meet at earlier.

***

Emma parked the car and walked over to the open area in the park. The snow-covered ground lit up as the moonlight shone down on it. "Micah?" she called out, looking around the park.

"Hi, beautiful," he whispered, sneaking up behind her. "I've missed you so much." As he tried to kiss her neck, she pulled away from him. "You okay?"

"Yeah. No. Micah, I don't know."

"What's going on?"

"I just learned everything. It's a lot of shit to process."

He looked at her, confused. "Everything? What do you mean?"

"Look, don't play dumb with me."

"Emma, I…" he began.

"So, when you're on the phone and suddenly get

off when I enter a room…how is Sebastian?"

"Sebastian?" His voice cracked.

"Yeah, I know about my father. Sebastian Blackwood."

Micah stepped back from her and began to breathe rapidly. "I…I don't know what you're talking about…"

"Don't lie to me, Micah!" Emma shouted.

"Look, I only knew him by Mr. Blackwood. I really wasn't on a first name basis with him."

"So, it's true? You've been working for my dad?" Emma breathed. The thought of even having this conversation with Micah made her stomach turn.

"Emma, calm down. I can explain." He grabbed her hands, trying to pull her toward him.

"Micah, I don't know if I want to hear it. Was everything we did so you could bring me to him? Was everything that we did just for a paycheck?"

"What? No! I mean, I was supposed to get close to you and bring you to him. But, I started to really fall for you. I can't put you in danger!" Micah grabbed her hands, squeezing tightly. He tried to pull her close to him, but she planted her feet.

"Oh, fuck off! You think I'm going to believe that now? And what about Kyle? Did you make him sick at the club the night of your opening?" Emma pulled her hands away from him and began to walk away.

"I…I didn't directly, Felix did…Emma, please don't go. I'm telling you the truth. I just wanted to keep you to myself and I knew Kyle wasn't really digging the idea of you with me."

"So, you're supposedly telling me the truth now, but everything else you told me was a lie? Classic. Look, Micah, I don't care what you run back to your 'boss' and tell him, but I don't want to see you. Ever. Again."

"Emma?"

"Goodbye, Micah," she whispered, walking away. He began to chase after her and she shot him back with her powers. As she returned to the car, the tears began to prick at her eyelids. To think she was really falling for him and he was the one leading her to the man who wanted her dead.

Micah had tried calling her three times as she drove home and left one voicemail. "Emma, I'm so sorry. Please talk to me. I really didn't mean…I've really fallen for you. I want nothing more than to protect you now! *Please* talk to me."

Once Emma got home, her mom had already gone to bed. She went straight to her room and began to cry herself to sleep. Today was a really long day and she was emotionally exhausted. To think, she wanted more than a normal life. Now, she'd kill for that normalcy. Crawling into her bed, she pulled the covers over her head and closed her eyes.

Chapter Seventeen

"Emma? Are you awake?" her mom asked, knocking on the bedroom door.

"Yeah, c'mon in." Emma had been awake for a few hours now. She had slept like shit, if she slept at all. She had only been with Micah for a short time, but it felt like they had connected. And no matter how short of a time they were together, finding out that he had been deceiving her still hurt.

"I had an idea."

"Mom, I really just wanna hang out in bed today."

"I'm not going to allow this moping around. You need to work on your magic and I know the best place."

"I'm not moping! I'm simply just…"

"You're moping," she interrupted. "So get your ass outta bed and shower. We leave in forty minutes."

"Ugh! All right," Emma huffed, throwing the covers to the side.

"Don't get huffy with me. I have coffee

downstairs, so hurry up."

Stomping past her mom, she hurried into the bathroom. The word 'coffee' always made her move a little faster. Emma quickly showered and got ready. She ran downstairs to find a fresh pot of coffee on the counter. She poured the to-go cup full and found her mom waiting for her in the living room, reading a book.

"All right, I'm ready. Where are we going?" Emma asked, sipping the coffee.

"You'll see," she said, setting down her book on the coffee table. She stood up and grabbed her coat and scarf. Emma set her cup down too and slipped on her coat and scarf.

"You know, if you really wanted—you could make the weather a bit nicer," she joked, picking her cup back up.

"You're funny. I have *some* control over the weather, I don't have *full* control. That means you're stuck." She laughed, opening the door.

The snow was slowly falling on them as they walked outside to the car. Her mom dusted off the car with the brush as Emma started the engine, blasting the heat. Moping or not, Emma really wanted to get back into her warm bed. If what her mom said was true—that Emma had all sorts of powers—she wondered if she could try to control some of the weather. Could she make it stop snowing? Could she maybe bring rain to those who needed it? So much was to be learned. Her mom opened the car, quickly sitting in the driver's seat, rubbing her hands together to warm them up.

She backed out of the driveway and drove down

206

the road. Emma watched the small old houses along the road pass by. The town had tried to restore a lot of the homes to look like they were built in the 1700s. Emma loved the historic feel of the town. She suddenly realized they were heading toward the bookstore.

It had been years since Emma had been there; she remembered going all the time as a kid. Emma loved the smell of the old books her mom had throughout the store. As Emma got older, she didn't really go as much. She always had something going on with her lacrosse games or some sort of debate to attend. Pulling into the parking lot outside the small building, the sign on the top of the building simply read *'Bookstore'*, nothing more. Her mom unlocked the front door, flipping the sign to *'open'*, and walked in. The familiar smell of the old books hit Emma as she walked through the door.

The building wasn't very big, but her mom had shelves with rows of books scattered around the store. As Emma walked around, looking through the selections, none of the books had a familiar author. Emma picked out a book that had some sort of foreign language written on the cover.

"That's a good one," her mom said, walking up next to her.

"You can read that?" Emma asked, pointing to the foreign script.

"It's Egyptian. My parents traveled a lot, so I know a few different languages."

"Wow, I didn't know that! So, what is this?"

"It's about Egyptian witchcraft. They study mostly about the Earth. They believe in Mother

Earth and how her powers are passed on to us."

"This really isn't your ordinary bookstore, is it?"

"No. I carry books that have beliefs, legends, and spells. Anything that you wanted to know about witchcraft, I have."

"You get a lot of business?"

"Just because a person isn't really a witch per se, they still love reading about it. For those who do have powers, they can try to learn more about them from these books."

"Like me."

"Exactly." Her mom nodded. Emma was now, more than ever, fascinated with the bookstore.

Emma set the book back on the shelf and began to browse through more of the collection. She found books on healing and wellness and pulled them from the shelf, and then walked over to the next set of books. *How To Control Your Powers* was the next book she picked up.

After grabbing several more, Emma took a seat at a table in the back corner. As Emma began to read, her mom tended to a couple of tourists who wanted to know if the store had any books on the Salem Witch Trials.

With each book she skimmed through, Emma was amazed to learn more about herself. But these books were written hundreds and even thousands of years ago. Witchcraft was in her blood, and yet she was only just learning about her powers. Her life was going to change so much.

***

For the next couple of days, Emma and her mom worked day and night on strengthening Emma's powers. On Christmas morning, they took a short break, continuing their tradition of a pancake breakfast and exchanging gifts. Emma hadn't heard from Micah at all, not that she wanted to, but it was weird not hearing from him. Emma was able to buy her mom a few small things during their trip to New York. The best gift that her mom gave her was an old book she had brought down from her closet. The book contained some spells and a history of her family and their powers. It was written by Emma's great-grandmother, and was almost like a diary. This was by far her favorite gift. As they took a break for lunch, Emma buried her face in the book. It had so many interesting facts about her family being put on trial during the Salem Witch debacle. Even though they were in fact witches, they were let off because of no true evidence. Her great-grandmother said they had used their powers to get off. It was incredible reading about all the history.

They continued their training after lunch, where her mom would put Emma's powers to work. She started off simple, helping her move objects across the table. Since she was a healer and Emma had the ability, her mom wanted to help Emma work on her healing powers. Emma thought her mom had lost her mind when she cut her finger on the edge of a small razor blade and then quickly healed herself. It was amazing to see her mom in action. She then put Emma to work. It took a few tries, but she finally was able to close up the wound.

Using her powers was mentally exhausting, but

in the end, Emma started to feel a bit more powerful. She would now be able to protect her mom, just like her mom had done for her.

Unfortunately, the twenty-eighth came too soon. As much as Emma was ready to be back in Denver, she wasn't sure that she truly wanted to leave her mom yet. "Em, are you all set? We need to leave," her mom called from the bottom of the stairs. Connor had come over to make the drive with them. Her mom and Connor had been talking every day since the trip to New York.

Emma's mom was worse than a teenager with a crush, constantly giggling on the phone with him. Connor was in town for the rest of the week and offered to take the drive with her.

Looking around the room, making sure nothing was left behind, Emma saw the bracelet on her dresser—her mom had put it back together. Picking it up and giving it a squeeze, Emma set it back down. She grabbed her bag and headed downstairs.

Connor offered to drive so Emma's mom wasn't driving while she was upset. The drive was rather silent. Grace said she didn't want to talk because she would only cry. Emma couldn't blame her, she would've probably cried too if they were to talk about her leaving. They dropped Emma off at the terminal, and her mom hugged her tightly. "I'll call you when I land," Emma said, starting to cry.

"Be safe. If you need anything, call me, okay?" Her mom wept.

"I will, Mom. I love you." She pulled away. "Connor, thank you for driving out with her. Take care of her, okay?"

"Will do. Safe travels. It was really nice to meet you," Connor said, handing Emma one of her bags.

"It was nice to meet you too. I'll see you guys later!" Emma plastered on a smile and headed inside. Turning around, she waved one last time before she walked down to the ticket counter. After checking her bags, her phone buzzed in her pocket. "Hello?"

"Hey, loser, what up?" Kyle joked.

"Do you know how much I've missed hearing your lame voice?" Emma laughed. It really was good to hear his voice.

"What're you doing?"

"I'm at the airport, heading home," she said excitedly. As much as it pained her to say goodbye to her mom, it was time to go to *her* home.

"Seriously? Sweet. The place isn't the same without you!" he exclaimed.

"What? You're home?" Emma asked excitedly.

"Yeah, I couldn't be at my mom's another minute. I needed to get out of there."

"Oh my God! That just made my day! I can't wait to see you! I have so much shit to tell you." Kyle really was going to shit himself hearing all the news of what she'd learned.

"Is Micah coming over?" he asked skeptically.

"We're done," she sighed.

"Oh shit. I'm sorry, Em. Wanna talk?" Kyle was always Emma's rock, especially when it came to heartache.

"No. I'm over it. Don't worry, you'll hear *all* about it later."

"Good. I don't know if I really want to hear it

now. I never liked him."

"Really? You guys seemed like you could be besties," Emma joked.

"And do our hair and talk about girls together?" Kyle said flamboyantly.

"Exactly!" She laughed. Kyle always made a good situation out of a shit one.

"You're a dick," he chuckled.

Emma gasped. "Did you seriously just call me a dick? You know I'm a chick, right?"

"Yeah, I know…but, you're still a dick." He laughed.

"Pizza tonight?" Emma asked excitedly as her stomach began to growl.

"You read my mind!"

"Yeah, you have no idea." She grabbed her stomach. Emma needed to think about something else as she was making herself hungrier.

"How about I pick you up from the airport and we'll go out," he suggested.

"Sweet! I'll see you in about four hours."

"Later, chick," he said before hanging up.

It was so nice to have Kyle to go home to. Emma was going to burst if she had to wait for him to come home after the new year.

Waiting for her plane, Emma tried playing several games on her phone. She could see why so many people complained about being addicted, they were horrible. Just when she thought she was getting ahead, her phone buzzed with an incoming message.

Micah: We need to talk. It's important.

Ugh. Micah. Emma typed out a response, regretting every second, but it was apparently important.

Emma: Go ahead. Tell me.

A moment after sending the message, Micah was calling. "What?" she answered

"Where are you?" he asked.

"Getting ready to board. I'm going home."

"I'll meet you later at your place," he insisted.

"No, you won't. I don't want to see you."

The line went dead. Emma was disappointed that she'd even given him the minute to speak. Why did she even bother picking up? Emma guessed a part of her really wanted to hear his voice. The attendant then came over the intercom and announced it was time to board.

***

As Emma rode the escalator in Denver International, she saw Kyle holding a sign up in the air. *'Emma the Dick'*. She couldn't help but laugh. The look on people's faces around them as they saw the sign was even more priceless.

"You're such an ass," Emma chuckled, smacking his arm.

"You didn't like the sign? It took me all day to make it!"

"All day? You've only just known I was coming home before I boarded! C'mon, my bags should be coming up, and I'm *starving.*" Walking toward the baggage claim, Kyle was hit on by a redhead, which gave them more to joke about. It was so great to be around her best friend again.

"How was the flight?" he asked, looking at the piece of paper that had the redhead's number.

Emma searched through the massive piles of baggage on the carousel. "It was smooth. I'm so glad to be home."

"Hey, speaking of home...do you know what happened to most of the coffee mugs?" he asked, grabbing her bags as she pointed them out.

"Uh...yeah...that's part of the long story I have to fill you in on." Emma sighed. They began to walk to the parking lot.

"Do I really want to know?" He laughed.

"Well, you know how you said I need to talk to my mom about what was going on?"

"Oh, yeah! So, what is it?" he asked eagerly.

"I...I'll tell you the whole story when we're sitting down...it's a lot."

"Shit. Everything okay?" he asked, stopping in the middle of the parking lot.

"Yes and no. God, you're impatient!" Emma grabbed one of her bags from him and headed to his SUV.

"Well, if you didn't have a million and a half things!"

"Shut your face! Let's go!" She laughed.

Kyle loaded the bags into the car. They drove toward their apartment, stopping at a pizzeria that was close to them. He continued to press for information, but she told him to wait until he at least had one beer in him. Once he finished his first beer, Emma began to retell the story her mom had told her, pausing to take bites of pizza. Emma could tell he wanted to ask a million questions as she told him, but he only sat there, listening. Once she was done, his jaw was hanging open and she couldn't wait to hear what he had to say. Emma then went into how she found out that Micah was working for her dad. "You okay? I expected you to at least talk shit. Even something along the lines of, 'I always knew you were a witch,' but nothing?"

"Emma, I'm actually speechless. I don't even know *what* to say," Kyle said, still trying to take in all the information.

"It's a lot, so you know how I felt hearing all this." She took a long drink of her beer.

"So, what are you gonna do?" he asked, signaling the waitress for another beer.

"I guess nothing? Maybe be ready for him?" Emma shrugged. What was she going to do? Emma hadn't even thought that far.

"This is some crazy shit. I know my mom, when I was a teenager, would say she was gonna kill me. Never once did she really mean it. Here you are, and your dad *actually* wants to kill you..." He paused.

"Yeah..." Emma sighed.

"And Micah was helping him?"

"Yep. I broke up with him, and I don't want him around!" she reassured him.

"Don't worry, I don't want the douche around anyway. I never did like him. Are you gonna kill him?"

"Micah?" Emma screeched.

215

"No, your dad." The waitress brought Kyle's beer and set it on the table. He quickly took a drink as he waited for Emma to answer.

Was she really going to kill her own dad? He did want to kill her… "No! Kyle, that's still *murder*!" Emma said quietly, looking around the restaurant. Not a subject she really wanted people hearing.

"This is fucked up."

"You're telling me," Emma breathed, stuffing the last bite of pizza in her mouth.

"Wanna go out tonight? I'll get ya really drunk and you can forget about it."

"Kyle, it's not something I'm gonna forget any time soon. I'm really tired and ready to go home."

"All right. I've got beer at home. I'll go pay, then we can head out." Kyle stood up and walked over to the young girl at the register and paid for their tab.

"Great. I'll head out to the car." Emma slipped on her coat and walked to Kyle's SUV.

Kyle ran to his car and they made their way back to the apartment. It was so nice to walk into her own home. She had yet to tell him about the whole losing her job thing. She didn't even know how to approach the subject.

"Hey, Ky?" Emma started nervously.

"Hey, Em?" he mocked.

"I…uh…I need to find a new job." Her stomach twisted in knots. It was bad enough that Kyle was paying for a bit more of the rent, but now Emma was out of a job.

"What? Why? What happened to the coffee shop?"

"I kinda quit."

"Jesus," Kyle sighed.

"I'm so sorry. I just…I'll find something fast and I'll ask my mom for money. I just wanted to give you a heads-up."

"You're lucky I like you." Kyle's grip on the steering wheel tightened. Emma felt horrible that she was dropping all of this information in his lap.

"I know, I'm really lucky."

"The receptionist position just opened up at work," Kyle informed her.

"Wait, I thought that was Phil's wife?"

"It was. I guess she was fucking around on him with some other dude. Anyway, Phil needs to fill it really fast. He's losing his mind answering the phones." He chuckled.

"I'll take it!" Emma screeched.

"All right, I'll give Phil a call when we get home."

Emma sighed with relief. It became quite clear that this year was going to be a whole new start.

Once they pulled into the parking garage of their complex, it felt so good to be home. The walk down memory lane was nice, but this was now her home. As soon as they walked in, Emma rushed into her room and threw herself on the bed. Her pillow had a vague smell of Micah's cologne. She quickly took off the pillow case, throwing it into her laundry basket.

The remainder of the night was spent doing piles of laundry and watching reruns of *The Simpsons*. As Emma watched one last episode, putting her clothes away, Kyle knocked on her door. "Okay, you start on Monday," Kyle said, poking his head into the room.

"Seriously? No interview?" Emma asked, surprised.

"He said he knows you well enough. As long as you don't fuck up, you're in with him."

"Wow! This is so cool! Thank you so much, Kyle!" Emma screeched, running over to him and hugging him tightly.

"Wow, I knew you wanted me, but this is a little much."

"Oh, shut up, pig!" Emma shouted, pushing him away. "I don't want you. I think that I'd rather be celibate for a year before sleeping with you."

"Ouch, I'm not that bad," he said, grabbing his chest.

"I don't wanna even find that out. Thank you for getting me the job, though. I really do appreciate it."

"Hey, now that you have a big girl job, maybe you can get a car?"

"Why? I can just ride with you!" Emma joked. But he was right, she could now have her own car. She became a little excited at the thought.

"You can ride with me until you start getting a paycheck. If I have to drive any more than that, though, you'll have to put out."

"Kyle! What is with all this sex talk?"

"I haven't been laid in a week," he sulked.

"What? Shit, is hell freezing?"

"Yeah, I think it is."

"Don't you have a list of skanks?"

"Yeah. I guess I'll start going through the list."

"Please do," she laughed. "I love you, Kyle, but eww."

Kyle smiled and headed to his room as Emma closed her door. She sorted through the laundry that she needed to do in the morning, then lay down on her bed. Thoughts of Micah fogged her head. Should she have listened and forgiven him? She shook her head—he was working for a man who wanted to kill her. Emma still checked her phone to see if she had any other missed calls or messages from him. Nothing. She really missed hearing his voice, but she needed to get some sleep so she could try and get him out of her head.

***

"My beautiful Emma. I love you. I wish you could see that." Micah sat on the edge of the chair.

"Micah, you've been sent to find me by the one person who wants me dead. How can you sit there and tell me that you love me?"

"Emma, when he sent me...I didn't expect to fall for you."

"Micah, I can't do this." Emma began to sob.

"I need to protect you." Micah reached for her hands.

"We can't be together..."

"I know...I just..."

"Micah..."

"We will be happy in the end. I will help you destroy him and then we can be happy together."

"Destroy him?" Emma asked, puzzled.

"Yes, you'll need to kill him to..." His voice began to fade.

"Em?" Kyle asked, knocking on her door. She grumbled as he opened the door. "Hey, I was getting ready to leave for work but I wanted to give you your Christmas present."

"Kyle, it's only seven," Emma complained.

"Hey, you're gonna have to get used to being up with the rest of us 'normal' folk. Work starts at eight."

Growling at him, she sat up. "Fine. What'd you get me?"

"Open it and see!" he said happily, handing her a small box. She ripped off the ribbon and inside was an ID bracelet.

"Oh, Kyle. I love it! Thanks!"

"Read what it says."

"B.F.F.F.L? Umm, Kyle, you had too many F's added."

"No, I didn't. It's 'best friends for fucking life.'" He laughed.

"You're such a dork!" She giggled. "Well, I had your gift emailed to me, so let me forward it. Hang on…" Emma grabbed her phone off the charger. It had a message waiting for her, but she bypassed it and forwarded the email that confirmed the concert tickets she purchased before she had left. "Okay, sent."

Kyle quickly pulled his phone out of his pocket. "No shit! Maroon 5 tickets? You're fucking awesome!"

"I got lucky getting them, but I knew that you loved them."

"Hell yeah. We still have a little while until the concert, but we'll have a great time! Oh shit, I gotta go. I'll see you after work?"

"Yeah, I'll be here."

"See ya!" Kyle said, dashing out of her room.

Emma figured since she was awake, it was time to start doing laundry and cleaning. She picked her phone up off the bed to check her messages.

Micah: I miss you, Emma.

Micah. Part of her missed him too, but she had to be strong. She needed to just ignore him. They were done and she had nothing more to say to him.

Chapter Eighteen

Having three days off before starting a new job was actually really nice. Emma missed working and getting out of the house, but it gave her time to work more on her powers and keep them under control. On Friday morning, nothing seemed to go her way. Emma ran out of laundry soap, Micah had texted her three more times with the same message, '*I miss you*,' and the coffee pot stopped working. Emma's powers were really being tested. Saturday was so much better. Her mom had sent her a large package of books, putting a note in each one, explaining how they could help her with her powers.

Emma spent the rest of the day locked up in her room, reading. She was thankful for the Internet so she could translate some of the scriptures, and she was intrigued by the history and knowledge of others that were in each book. Emma had been reading for most of the night, and Kyle had gone out with some old college friends, so it gave her a little peace and quiet.

Sunday, the two of them slept in and lounged around the apartment. Kyle was sweet enough to order them some Chinese food for dinner. "You ready to start bright and early tomorrow?" Kyle asked, flipping through channels.

"Yeah, I think so," Emma mumbled, shoveling the last potsticker into her mouth.

"I'm pretty sure when Damon heard that you were coming to work with us, everyone saw his boner."

"What?" Emma laughed.

"You know, an *erection*," Kyle explained.

"I know what a boner is." She shook her head, smacking her forehead with the palm of her hand.

"I think he likes you."

"I'm not ready to date again."

"Who said date?" he joked.

"Ugh." Emma rolled her eyes and crossed her arms. She began to pout; how was it that Kyle had no problems breaking up with girls and only using them for sex? As they started to watch a show about the dumbest people on the planet—doing stupid shit that made her cringe—a knock at their door scared her.

"You expecting anyone?" Kyle asked. Emma shook her head, but her heart stopped at the thought of it being Micah. Kyle got up and walked to the front door. Once he opened the door, Emma could hear a girl's voice coming in through the hallway. "Em, this is Karen."

"Hi," Emma said, waving to the beautiful blonde. Her blue eyes were sparkling. She was easily five-eight, with long legs, and a million dollar smile. She and Kyle looked like an All-American couple in a GAP ad with their matching blond hair and blue eyes.

"Hi, Emma. Nice to meet you," Karen said sweetly.

Emma about died. A girl here for Kyle who didn't feel some sort of threat and was actually willing to say hi? "Do you want to sit down, Karen?" Emma offered.

"We're gonna go hang out in my room," Kyle interrupted.

"Well, I'm going to bed. I'll see you in the morning?" Emma said, turning off the television.

"Yep. See ya." Kyle had a cheesy grin on his face as he escorted Karen to his bedroom. Emma picked up the empty Chinese cartons and tossed them in the trash.

"Nice to have met you, Emma," Karen said.

"You too, Karen," Emma responded.

Emma waved to the two of them and went into her room, shutting the door behind her. Turning on the TV, Emma went through her clothes to find an outfit for her first day. She went with some red slacks and a black button-down shirt, laying them out on her desk. Emma snapped her fingers and lit the candles on her dresser when her phone began to ring. An unknown number came across her screen. "Hello?" she asked.

"Emma?" Micah said.

"Micah, what do you want?" She sighed.

"I just wanted to hear your voice. I'm...I miss you."

"Micah, you betrayed me."

"I know. I'm sorry. I need to talk to you, though."

"About what?" Emma was kicking herself for answering the phone.

"Can I see you?"

"Micah. I'm getting ready for bed. Just tell me."

"No. Meet for lunch?"

"I can't…" Emma sighed.

"Dinner, then. I'll pick you up at seven," he stated before she hung up on him.

Setting her alarm, Emma crawled into bed, and the sound of moaning suddenly filled her room.

"Ugh! Not my night!" Emma huffed, turning up the television. She couldn't help but begin to wonder if meeting Micah was a ploy, and her heart began to race. What if he was setting her up? Especially since Micah couldn't tell her over the phone. Emma pulled out one of the books her mom had sent, trying to take her mind off everything.

As her eyes began to get heavy, she looked at the time and saw it was already three in the morning. She tossed the book onto the floor and cuddled into her pillow.

***

Even after little sleep, once her alarm went off, Emma was more than willing to actually wake up early. She even beat Kyle to making coffee. He was a little worried that something was wrong with her since she was up early and functioning properly.

Once they got to the office, Kyle briefly showed her the breakroom and then brought her back to

Phil's office. Phil had most of the pictures lying face down around the office. The only pictures that were still standing were of him and his dog. Kyle informed Emma before they got to the office that Phil was really bitter about the divorce and not to bring it up. Phil re-introduced himself before briefly filling her in on his 'whore of a wife' and how she was going to regret cheating on him. Emma quickly tried to change the subject to how she wanted a tour of the office. Nothing was more awkward than hearing him talk about his pending divorce on her first day.

"So, this is your desk," Phil said, gesturing to the desk in the middle of the office. "If you need anything, just holler."

"Thank you so much, Phil. I really appreciate you giving me the job."

"Yeah, no problem. I think you'll fit right in." He smiled and walked into his office as Emma sat down at her new desk, sending her mom a text.

Emma: Started my job! Already have my own desk LOL. I'll call you on my lunch.

Setting her phone on the desk, the office phone began to ring. Emma froze. She didn't even know what greeting to use. Looking over at Phil's office, he was on a call. A deep voice then answered the phone, Emma turned in her chair to see Damon standing in front of her desk.

"Denver Press, Damon speaking. Yep, let me transfer you." He pressed *transfer* and dialed a few numbers, then hung up.

226

"Thank you. I guess I forgot to ask what to say." Emma laughed.

"No worries. How you liking it so far?" Damon asked, smiling widely at her.

"Well...I just got here about fifteen minutes ago, so I'd say not bad." She nervously chuckled.

"Yeah, I guess I should've saved that question for the end of the day." He playfully smacked his forehead.

"Probably. I'll pretend you didn't ask it," Emma joked. She could tell he was trying his best to flirt, but it wasn't going according to plan. She couldn't help but feel bad.

"Thanks. Hey, you got plans for lunch?" he asked, fidgeting with his bag.

"Not as of yet," Emma said, blushing.

"Good. We'll go to this Chinese restaurant right around the corner, their egg rolls are amazing. My treat," he insisted.

"I don't know how long I have though," Emma answered hesitantly. She hadn't even been here an entire day and she was already being asked out? She blushed a little more.

"I'll say it was a business meeting, you can have an hour." He was very persistent.

"You're gonna get me fired!" Emma exclaimed.

"Nah, Phil is pretty cool. As long as you're not gone all day and answer the phone at least a few times...so, you game?"

"Sure," she agreed.

"Great, I'll meet you up here about one." He smiled widely.

"Okay." She couldn't believe that she was

227

already giving in to a lunch date, but who could blame her? His smile was killer and his blue eyes were entrancing.

"Oh, that paper over there," he pointed to the slip of paper next to the phone, "it has everyone's extension. Just press *transfer* and their extension. We all have voicemail, so don't worry about taking messages."

"Thanks, Damon," she said, going over the list of numbers. He waved as he walked to his desk. Having him around was going to make it hard to work here. Her cell phone vibrated on the desk, scaring her back to reality.

Mom: Good luck, honey! I can't wait to hear all about it! LOVE YOU.

The morning began to fly by as Emma got acquainted with the copy machine and phone system. She never thought that office equipment would hate her so much. She hung up on a few people, but once she explained it was her first day, they were a little sympathetic. Kyle stopped by a few times to make sure everything was going okay, but the phone was ringing off the hook, so she couldn't really talk to him. He reassured her it was only on Mondays that it was this crazy, but the rest of the week was pretty lax.

"Emma, if you'd like, you can take your lunch," Phil said, tapping on her desk. She looked down at the time, the clock read twelve forty-five.

"Thanks, Phil. How long do I get?"

"Go ahead and take an hour. I have a meeting, so

228

I'll be gone for the rest of the day. If you have any problems, I told Kyle to help you out…" He paused, looking around her desk. "How do you like it so far?"

"I had to get used to the phone ringing constantly and I think the copier hates me, but I think I'm going to enjoy it." She chuckled.

"Well, I'm glad. Have a good night," Phil said, tapping her desk once more.

"You too."

"You ready for lunch?" Damon said, walking toward her desk.

"I am! Let me lock my computer and grab my coat out of the breakroom."

"I'll grab it," he offered.

"Thanks."

He hurried around the corner to the breakroom, bringing her black coat back with him. She slipped it on and grabbed her purse. Her stomach had been growling since nine in the morning, and Emma decided she was going to have to learn to eat breakfast. Only having coffee at seven in the morning was *not* going to cut it. Damon and Emma walked around the corner to a tiny Chinese café. As he opened the door for her, the aroma from all the food was fantastic.

They sat down in a corner booth and the hostess handed them some paper menus. Emma looked over the small menu, deciding on the Mongolian beef and the egg rolls that Damon insisted were the best. As she set the menu down on the table, she got a paper cut. "Shit!"

"You okay?" he asked, holding out his hand to

see.

"Yeah, I'm fine. Paper cuts are the worst!"

He grabbed her hand and pulled her finger up to his mouth, placing a soft kiss on the cut.

Emma's heart melted as she watched his soft lips pull away from her hand. "Better?" he asked.

"Y-yes," she stuttered, blushing. She'd never been so turned on by a kiss on the finger. She quickly forgot about the pain from the cut.

"I'll be right back, I need to run to the restroom." He released her hand with one last kiss as he stood from the booth.

Emma nodded, smiling as she rubbed her finger, and suddenly her cut began to disappear. Even though she was relieved the cut was gone, she was now going to have to try to explain that to Damon. As their waitress passed her, Emma asked for a bandage and she hurried to the hostess stand, bringing back a tiny bandage. Emma quickly put it on before Damon returned.

***

Lunch was amazing, and getting to know Damon was equally as nice. He was such a gentleman. When they returned to work, the rest of the day was a breeze and Kyle finally appeared from his paper-stacked desk at five fifteen.

"Sorry, Em. I had so much shit to get done today. You ready to go?"

"Yep," she said, gathering up her things.

"How'd your first day go?" he asked, putting on his jacket.

"Not bad. I like it!"

"Good, and hey, I heard you went out to lunch with Damon," he said, winking.

"Wow, you're all a bunch of gossips!" Emma laughed.

"Pretty much. Just don't tell any secrets to our gossip columnists, they'll print that shit," he joked.

"Seriously?"

"Yeah, it's been slow," he said, shaking his head. "They'll take anything right about now. How about a beer?"

"I'm gonna have to pass. I need to get home and..." She stopped. She didn't know how to even tell Kyle she was meeting Micah.

"And what?"

"Don't be mad, but I told Micah I'd meet him for dinner," she said hesitantly.

"What!" Kyle yelled.

"Shh! We'll talk more on the way home."

Kyle rolled his eyes as they walked out to the parking lot. He was silent during the drive home, but as soon as they pulled into their parking lot, he looked at her, waiting for an explanation.

"So?" he huffed.

"He called last night and said he really needed to talk to me and he won't seem to tell me anything over the phone."

"Emma, he just wants to fuck with your head."

"Kyle, I don't think so. Besides, I'm a lot stronger with...with everything, and I can take care of myself."

"Be careful, Emma. I don't trust him. Promise me, if you need anything you'll call me. I'll be there in a flash!"

"I will, and I promise."

"Since he's betrayed you before, what if your dad is with him?"

"Then it will be an awkward family reunion!" Emma joked, but she really didn't know what she would do if Micah showed up with her dad.

"I'm serious, Em."

"Me too," she deadpanned before getting out of the car. They walked up to the apartment and Kyle's phone began to ring.

"It's Karen," he sighed.

"Well, answer it! I kinda liked her, she seemed...normal."

"That's the thing, she is."

"And it's a problem?" Emma asked.

"In a way...yes."

"You're gonna have to explain that one, then."

"She's not looking for a relationship. And for once she's actually really smart, not a dumb blonde. Right now, all Karen wants is to just hang out and have sex. Emma, she's me. With boobs. I'm actually...in lust! And since she doesn't want all this, I do!"

Emma began to laugh hysterically. Kyle had finally met his match. "You're insane, but I gotta say...don't let her go! Keep her around for a bit."

"I guess you're right. We'll see." Kyle called her back and went straight to his room, closing the door behind him. Emma went to her room and set down her things just as her phone began to ring. It was her mom.

"Oh shit, I forgot to call you on lunch!" Emma

cried as she answered the phone.

"I figured you got busy. How was it?" she asked excitedly.

"I really liked it. A lot of nice people and a guy…" Emma said hesitantly.

"Emma…" she sighed.

"No, he's a nice guy! And he's not magical!" Emma laughed. "Oh! I wanted to share, I healed a paper cut really fast!"

"That's great! You're going to notice a lot more happening. Just be careful, okay?"

"I will. Well, I'm going to eat some dinner and then call it an early night. I'm not used to waking up early."

"That's really great. How's the reading coming along?" her mom asked, changing the subject.

"It's going really well. It's all so…interesting. I can't believe a lot of the things I'm reading about are actually real."

"Do you have any questions?"

"Not right now, I'm just really enjoying learning."

"I'm proud of you. Call me later."

"Okay, Mom. I love you." Emma's heart warmed that she was able to have this new bond with her mom.

"Love you too." She hung up and Emma sat on the edge of her bed. Micah said seven, but she was already starving. She was half-tempted to eat now and then she could leave sooner. As Emma considered what to do, her phone rang again.

She answered the call, but before she could say anything, Micah asked, "Are you ready?"

"I thought you said seven."

"I did, but I thought my meeting was going to be a little longer. I can be there in ten."

"All right, I'm ready. I'll meet you outside."

"That's fine. I'm on my way."

Emma hung up, then grabbed her coat and put it back on. As she came out of her room, Kyle was sautéing some peppers. "Yum, what're you making?" she asked, inhaling the smell.

"Bratwurst and peppers, want some?" Kyle offered, lifting the lid of the pan.

"I wish. I'm heading out. I'll be back in a couple hours."

"Call me if you need anything."

"Karen coming over?" Emma asked, winking.

"No, she said she's got some school function to chaperone."

"Stood up for a younger model? Damn, that's harsh," Emma joked.

"You're dumb. See ya. Oh, and tell dickhead if he hurts you—I'll fucking make him disappear."

"I will, see ya." Emma waved, closing the door behind her, and walked down the stairs, just as Micah pulled up.

He slid out of the driver's seat and walked around to the passenger door, opening it for her. "Thanks," she said quietly.

"You're welcome. Hungry?"

"Yeah." She didn't know what to say to him. This was such an awkward meeting.

"You look beautiful," Micah whispered.

"Look…" Emma started.

"What have you been up to?" he asked, trying to

grab her hand. She quickly put it in her lap.

"Micah, don't…"

"No, I shouldn't have tried. Sorry."

"So, what's going on?" she huffed. She was getting a little annoyed.

"I stopped working for your dad."

She turned to face him in her seat. "I'm sorry, what?"

"Yeah, I told him I couldn't work for him anymore. He didn't ask any questions, said he understood, and I left."

"Micah, I don't know my dad, but that seems too easy."

"He's not that bad. I hate to say it, but I did find out where you were…"

Emma glared at him. "What *did* you tell him?"

"That I found you in Denver. He wanted me to find out more about you…"

"And?"

"Well, I told him you didn't know much about your powers and that's it."

"So, how the hell did he get my number?" Emma snapped.

"That's why I couldn't talk to you on the phone. He gave me the phone when I started working for him and I think he tracked it."

"Micah! If he tracked it, he knows where I live! Can you stop the car?"

"I didn't mean he tracked it, but probably got your number off of it."

"Micah. Stop the car," Emma demanded.

"I thought we were going to dinner?"

"I really don't want to go out with you. I want

you to stop the car!" The car suddenly stalled.

"Emma…" Micah started. Emma grabbed her purse and opened the door. She needed to breathe.

"Emma, please don't leave. I miss you. I've never felt this way before. I'm not one to beg for someone to come back to me. You mean something to me," Micah begged.

"Micah…" She didn't even know how to respond. "I'm sorry," she said, walking away from him. The tears streamed down her face as she walked home.

Chapter Nineteen

The walk home was a rather cold one. Emma needed to clear her head of all things Micah. Just when she thought things were going to get better without him, he had to go and pull something like this. She began to cry; ugly cry. Her tears felt like they were going to freeze to her cheeks. As her apartment came into view, she pushed herself to walk a little faster. Her lungs were burning from the cold air, but all she wanted to do was get inside, get warm, and maybe punch something. Walking up to the entryway of her building, she wiped her tears on her jacket sleeve. Emma couldn't have Kyle seeing her this upset. He'd flip out and that was the last thing she needed. More drama. Emma raced up the stairs to her door, taking a deep breath as she tried to clear her head.

"Wow, I'd say that was a quickie!" Kyle retorted as she walked through the front door. He was lounging on the couch, watching some television.

"Shut up. Do you still have some peppers and bratwurst left over?" she asked, slamming the door behind her.

"You didn't even get a free meal?" he said, muting the TV and walking toward her. "Yeah, there's some in the pan."

"No, Kyle! I even walked home, I am so done with his shit!" Emma seethed.

"Why didn't you call? I would've come and picked you up." Kyle followed her into the kitchen, handing her a plate from the cabinet.

"I needed some time to clear my head." Emma grabbed a bun and loaded it with peppers and a sausage. She was so hungry that she took a bite that was way too big for her mouth.

"Well, no wonder he didn't want to eat with you." He grimaced as he watched her stuff her face.

"Shut your face!" she mumbled, trying to keep food from spilling out of her mouth. Kyle handed her a napkin from the counter as she walked by him on her way to the table.

"So, what happened?" Kyle asked.

"He wanted to tell me he stopped working for my dad and he misses me." She took another bite. "Then he went on about us being together and that my dad knows where I live."

"What the fuck? So, some crazy fucker knows where we live?"

Emma nodded as she chewed on her food. "Yep. Gonna sleep soundly tonight, huh?"

"Fuck! Emma, maybe…"

"What? Quit my job, move, and stay in hiding?"

Kyle shrugged. "I don't know, but sounds like the safe way to do things."

"Kyle, I'm going to keep living my life. If he

wants to battle, he's gonna have a great fight on his hands. I'm only gonna get stronger."

"That's what worries me." Kyle sighed.

"The fact that I'm actually gonna have to fight with powers against someone who has less powers?"

"Yeah, or even the fact that you're...that you have powers!"

"Don't worry. I've got it covered." Emma winked, shoving the last bite into her mouth.

"Well, you could just show him how unladylike you are and spark a bonding moment." Kyle laughed as he wiped her face with the napkin.

"You're a douche," Emma laughed. "All right, I'm gonna go to bed. I don't know how you've done this early-morning-thing since after college."

"It's called *growing up*. Sucks, don't it?"

"Yeah, it does!" Emma rolled her eyes.

"See ya bright and early!" Kyle walked in his room and shut the door behind him. Emma couldn't thank him enough for helping her get another job.

"Yaay!" she shouted sarcastically, walking to her room. Emma checked her phone before plugging it into the charger. Not one missed call or text from Micah. Maybe he finally took the hint. Shutting her door, she climbed into her bed. She could feel the tears building up, but she didn't want to waste anymore of her time crying over him.

***

The rest of the week was about the same. Emma did notice the phones slowed down as the week progressed, and she soon learned the extensions of everyone in the office. The same people seemed to receive the same calls every day. On Friday, everyone wore jeans and really dressed down. She was more than okay with that. Damon looked sexier than ever in jeans and a black thermal shirt. She felt flustered every time he walked by her desk. He wasn't on Phil's team, but he did occasionally work with Phil on ideas for stories. Which Emma also figured was a reason to walk by her desk.

At around two thirty, Emma came back from a late lunch and found a large bouquet of flowers sitting on her desk. She searched the bouquet for a card or envelope, but couldn't find one.

"I see you got my flowers," Damon said as he walked out of Phil's office.

She looked up at him, surprised. "You got me flowers? Why?"

"A beautiful woman deserves flowers for no special reason," he declared, winking.

"You really shouldn't have," she said, smiling widely.

"How do you feel about dinner tonight?"

"Well, I enjoy dinner every night," Emma joked.

"Touché. How about dinner with me?" he insisted, grabbing her hand. His thumb caressed her knuckles as he locked his eyes on hers.

"All right. Is it okay to wear jeans?" She pointed to her outfit. "Or should I go home and change?"

"No, what you have on is perfect. I was thinking casual anyway."

"So, after work?"

"Yeah, we can just go straight away."

240

"Great! See you later." She waved to him as she sat down and got back to work.

Damon walked back to his desk and she realized the flowers needed some water. She hurried into the breakroom and filled the vase. They really were beautiful flowers, but she felt like she was moving a little quick by going on dates with Damon. She had just broken up with Micah and now she was dating?

Sitting back down at her desk, her phone began to vibrate. Micah's number came up on the screen. She instantly pressed *ignore*. Why couldn't he just get the point? He betrayed her trust and she no longer wanted to be with him. The voice mail icon appeared on her screen. She was half-tempted to delete it, but she wanted to hear what he had to say.

"Emma, please talk to me. I've never been this way…"

She hung the phone up mid-sentence, then put her phone on silent and placed it in her purse. He needed to understand that she didn't want to be with him.

For the rest of the afternoon, Emma tried her hardest to put him in the back of her mind. She had a dinner to look forward to with Damon. On Fridays, the office left right at five, and she waved to everyone as they began to leave. Just as she started to turn off her computer, Damon walked up to her desk.

"You about ready?" Damon asked, slipping his bag over his shoulder.

"Yeah, I'll be ready in just a few. Let me go tell Kyle I don't need a ride."

"No need. We were talking earlier and I already

told him."

"Oh. Well, great. We can go, then."

Helping her into her coat, Damon grabbed her hand and led her to his car. A beautiful red BMW was parked in the back lot. Damon pressed a button on his remote and started the car. He winked as he opened the door for her, then slipped into the driver's seat and inserted the key into the ignition. "Hungry?" he asked.

"Actually, I am. Where are we going?" Emma asked, buckling her seatbelt.

"A little bar down the road. They have some really good food and I thought we'd get a beer or two, to celebrate your first week."

"Sounds good. I could use a beer...or two." She laughed.

As they drove down the road, that awkward silence filled the car. Although Damon was incredibly sexy and smooth, Emma wasn't feeling a connection with him. All she could do was think about Micah.

They pulled up to the bar, which seemed to be rather packed. She'd only seen it during the day and never thought anyone actually came to this place, there was never a car in its parking lot. Damon placed his hand on her back as they walked in, and she felt a bit of cold energy run up her spine. It was almost like she could sense a bit of evil about Damon as he touched her. Emma looked at him and saw him smiling widely at her. She felt a little unnerved by this feeling.

Sitting down in a booth away from the crowd, Damon slid in the seat next to her. A really busty waitress walked up to their table, squeezing her boobs together to grab Damon's attention—more than she already had. "What can I get you guys?" she asked in a high-pitched voice.

"I'll have a beer," Emma quickly said.

"Make it two," Damon added. The waitress smiled widely before she skipped away. "So, what're you hungry for?"

"The hot wings sound really good. I think I'm gonna try those. What about you?"

"I like the bacon cheeseburger."

"Yum, that does sound good." As Emma leaned over Damon to place the menu at the edge of the table, he kissed her cheek. She didn't know how to respond to it, so she just smiled at him.

"Sorry, I wanted to get that awkward kiss out of the way, so the next one will be amazing."

"Um...Damon..." As Emma started, their perky waitress brought the beers to the table.

"Are you guys wantin' to order some food?" she asked.

"Yeah, she's gonna have the hot wings and I'll have the bacon cheeseburger," Damon said, handing her the menus.

"Great, guys. By the way, I'm Angie—if you need anything."

"Thanks, Angie," Emma said politely.

Damon took a swig of his beer and as he set the glass back on the table, his hand rubbed Emma's left thigh. She was now starting to feel a little uncomfortable. "Damon?"

"Yeah?" he asked.

"Look, I'm so glad we're getting to hang out and

I really appreciate everything…I just don't want to move so fast. I just got out of a relationship."

"Fast? I'm not moving fast, Emma."

"Well, your hand would state otherwise." She tried pushing his hand off of her leg, but he began to squeeze tighter.

"Look, I think you owe me this."

"I *owe* you this?" Emma asked in shock.

"Yes. Every time we've talked, you seem to flirt with me and lead me on. Then, when you had a *boyfriend*, you still wanted to be around me, but you'd have your *boyfriend* step in to tease me."

"Damon, you have the wrong idea of me!"

His hand cupped the back of her head, pulling her onto his lips. She tried her hardest to push him away, but she didn't want to have to use her powers in the middle of a crowded bar. Instead, she grabbed her beer and poured it over his head, causing him to quickly stand up. "What the fuck!" he shouted, brushing the beer off his clothes.

"Keep your hands off me!" Emma seethed. The entire bar looked over at them as she grabbed her coat, storming out. Once Emma reached the outside, she let out a heavy sigh. What a jerk. Starting to walk down the street, a strong grip tightened around her arm.

"You fucking bitch!" Damon screamed. "Where the fuck do you think you're going?"

"I'm going home! Let go of me!" She began to feel her powers tingle at her fingertips.

He began to pull her toward him. "Our date isn't over yet!"

"Yeah, Damon—it is," she said calmly, using a

little bit of her power to push him away.

"What the hell was that?" he asked, surprised. Suddenly, Emma saw Micah walk up behind Damon.

"It was a nice way of telling you to leave her alone!" Micah yelled, pulling Damon toward him, punching him hard in the jaw.

"Micah? What are you doing here?" Emma screeched.

"Saving your ass. Go get in the car!" he ordered. Emma didn't argue with him, anywhere away from Damon was going to be better. She heard Damon yell something as she closed the door to the SUV, which he had left running. Emma watched out the car window as Micah punched Damon again before grabbing his head. Gritting his teeth, he told him something in his ear, then Micah jogged over to the driver's side of the SUV. He hurried in and began to drive off.

"Are you stalking me?" Emma asked, crossing her arms.

"Emma, I told you I need to protect you."

"So, that's a yes."

He ignored her last comment, changing the subject. "Why were you out with him? Didn't you listen to me when I told you he only wants to fuck you?"

"Yeah, 'cause you've been so honest about everything else, right?"

"Emma…"

"Can you please just take me home?"

"Yeah," he sighed.

Micah drove the short distance to her apartment.

He placed the SUV in park and started to get out. "What are you doing?" Emma asked.

"I'm going up with you. We need to talk."

"Micah, we're done."

"I understand. But it's not about us."

She let out a heavy sigh. "Fine." What a night. A guy she had thought was going to be a nice guy, actually turned out to be a total maniac, and the guy who was bad news, came to her rescue. She needed a drink.

As she walked through the door, Kyle was strutting around in his towel and Karen in his shirt. "Oh, shit. Sorry, Em, I thought you'd be home later!" Kyle exclaimed. Karen smiled embarrassedly and hurried toward Kyle's room, shutting the door.

"It's okay, long, fucking story…" Emma rolled her eyes as Micah walked in through the door behind her.

"What the hell is he doing here!" Kyle roared.

"Another long story. He and I need to talk."

"Emma, do you want me to stay here?" Kyle asked, completely ignoring Micah. Kyle began to walk toward Micah.

Emma put her arm out to stop him. "No, it's okay. Can you give us a sec alone?" she asked, facing Kyle. "Please, it's okay." Emma placed her hand on his shoulder. He looked at her and nodded before walking away to his room.

Emma turned back to Micah. "What is *so* important?"

"I can't stop thinking about you. I'm so sorry, Emma…" he started.

"For what? Lying to me? Working for a guy who

wants nothing more than to see me dead?" she interrupted.

"Everything. I miss hearing your voice…"

"Micah, if this was the important thing…I really don't want to hear it."

"No…" he began, but was interrupted by the ringing of his phone. Pulling out his cell phone, his face paled as he answered. "Yep. All right, hang on." He pulled the phone away from his ear and handed it to her. "It's for you…"

She looked at him strangely, hesitating to take the phone from his hand. "Hello?" she answered.

"Hello, Emma. I hope you're ready to die…" His words began to trail off and Emma started to feel light-headed.

Without any hesitation, she threw the phone across the room, before everything went black and she fell to the floor. Micah quickly grabbed her, holding her tightly in his arms. "Emma?" She could faintly hear him calling her name. "Emma?" His voice became louder and a little clearer. She felt like she was in a haze.

"Wh-hat?" Emma stuttered.

"You fainted! Are you okay? What did he say?" Micah panicked.

His face became blurred again, but she tried to focus in on him. "He wants to me to die…" she whispered before everything went black again.

To Be Continued…

Acknowledgements

This book was something completely out of the ordinary for me, so much so that I laughed when my mom said I should write a book about a witch. Well, now that I actually wrote it—thank you, Mom. I had so much fun writing this and cannot wait until the next book!

As always, thank you to my dear friend, Ying. You've help me more than you know and I really do appreciate you. You're a hard worker and it will never go unnoticed by me. I can't say thank you enough. You were there from the get-go and I'm so glad to have you by my side!

To my amazing husband, Hoss. Honey, I love you so much and I'm so glad you've supported me on my decision to write. Even if you get mad that I've stayed up really late 'finishing one last idea.'

Kids—Mommy loves you! Thank you for getting excited when I tell you my book is coming out soon.

To all the bloggers who I've bothered and stalked, asking to post my cover and teaser pics—thanks for putting up with me. Haha!

To the Limitless team—I'm so grateful to be a part of such an amazing team. Gillian, thank you for all your hard work, I appreciate your help!

And last but definitely not least, my amazing friends—I love you guys!

About the Author

Michelle Escamilla is a married mom of two. She began writing just to pass the time, waiting for one of her favorite authors to release her upcoming book, but soon found a new passion. When she is not writing, she is spending time with her kids, husband or family. She lives in Colorado, where she loves the Mountains during the summer months for hiking and would love to be on a beach during the winter months.

Facebook:
https://www.facebook.com/authormichellee

Twitter:
https://twitter.com/msescamilla

www.ingramcontent.com/pod-product-compliance
Lightning Source LLC
Chambersburg PA
CBHW020402120726
47904CB00002B/675